"You want me, o[...]
protect you?"

Vivian took a deep breath. She'd known coming here wouldn't be easy, but Joe was her best option and her first choice.

"I'm no longer entitled to Secret Service protection and I wouldn't want that anyway. I could hire another investigator but that person wouldn't know me and wouldn't really understand the situation like you do."

And the last time in her life she had felt truly safe was when Joe had been watching over her. She wanted that again. She was willing to sacrifice her pride to get it. Hers had been a foolish stunt by a twenty-year-old girl who thought she was madly in love...

You were *madly in love.*

Regardless, she thought, her feelings had cost him his job, his future and his relationship with his father. Not to mention what that did to the rest of his family. Vivian had considered what might happen when she saw him again—that he might yell or, worse, tell her to get lost in that scary soft tone he always used when he was super angry.

His laughter was unexpected.

Then suddenly he stopped. "You do recall what happened the last time you were under my protection?"

Dear Reader,

Her Secret Service Agent is kind of a crazy story. I actually wrote this book many, many years ago. And I always loved the idea of it. However, after taking it out of the drawer, I realized how much I had changed as a writer in the years since and knew that I was going to write the whole book over again.

It was great rediscovering my old self while at the same time realizing how far I had come in my twenty-plus years writing for Harlequin.

Joe was then and is now one of my most favorite heroes, and Vivian is the heroine I most respect for being afraid about a lot of things but always standing up to those fears. I really hope you enjoy their story! If you like *Her Secret Service Agent*, you can follow me on Amazon, find me at www.stephaniedoyle.net, on Facebook at Stephanie Doyle Books, or on Twitter, @stephdoylerw. Phew! That's a lot of places.

Stephanie

STEPHANIE DOYLE

Her Secret Service Agent

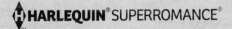 HARLEQUIN® SUPERROMANCE®

Recycling programs
for this product may
not exist in your area.

ISBN-13: 978-0-373-64033-1

Her Secret Service Agent

Copyright © 2017 by Stephanie Doyle

Printed in U.S.A.

www.Harlequin.com

Stephanie Doyle, a dedicated romance reader, began to pen her own romantic adventures at age sixteen. She began submitting to Harlequin at age eighteen and by twenty-six her first book was published. Fifteen years later, she still loves what she does, as each book is a new adventure. She lives in South Jersey with her cat, Hermione, the designated princess of the house. When Stephanie's not reading or writing, in the summer she is most likely watching a baseball game and eating a hot dog.

Books by Stephanie Doyle

HARLEQUIN SUPERROMANCE

The Bakers of Baseball

The Comeback of Roy Walker
Scout's Honor
Betting on the Rookie

The Way Back
One Final Step
An Act of Persuasion
For the First Time
Remembering That Night

HARLEQUIN ROMANTIC SUSPENSE

Suspect Lover
The Doctor's Deadly Affair

SILHOUETTE BOMBSHELL

Calculated Risk
The Contestant
Possessed

Visit the Author Profile page at Harlequin.com for more titles.

CHAPTER ONE

Ten Years Ago

"VIV, WHERE ARE we going?"

"Just follow me," Vivian said, taking Joe by the hand and leading him through the crowded house party a couple of blocks off the Georgetown campus. She needed privacy, something she'd thought would be easy to find at a college party. Everyone had stories about secret hookups at parties like this. The reality, however, was there were more people than space in the brownstone and the hooking-up seemed to happen openly.

Something she might have known if she actually did the college party scene more often. She didn't usually come to these types of events. Not the most social person, she preferred spending her nights quietly with a small circle of friends. Friends she could trust.

For that matter so did Joe Hunt, who was her Secret Service point man.

Tonight had been his night off, but Vivian had convinced him to switch shifts with Cindy, who mostly handled nights and weekends. Joe had a hard time denying Vivian anything, so it wasn't a surprise he'd agreed to the request. Now she had to work up the courage to go through with the rest of her plan.

Vivian thought that if she could have him to herself at a casual event, and they could really talk, then he might understand what she was feeling. He might also be more willing to admit what she was pretty sure he was feeling, too.

"Seriously, Viv, if this is about you thinking I'm going to let you drink, forget it. You've got six months to go before you're twenty-one, and I'm not bending on a single hour. Your father would have my ass."

Vivian didn't bother to answer. As if drinking beer was even close to what she was getting ready to tell him. She'd been waiting for this night for weeks, and the last person she wanted to think about now was Daddy.

As president of the United States, leader of the free world, he was known to be an overbearing hard-liner. As a single father to his only daughter, he was even stricter. He would definitely not approve of what Vivian was about to do.

Despairing of finding an empty bedroom, she decided her second-best option was a room she knew would allow them privacy and had a lock on the door. She found an upstairs bathroom off the master bedroom. While there were people milling about in the bedroom, talking and drinking, the bathroom was fortunately unoccupied.

It would have to do.

She pulled Joe in behind her, shut the door and locked it for good measure. Phase One was complete.

Then she turned to face him, and all the words got stuck in her throat. He was dressed casually, albeit professionally, to help blend in at the event. As point man, his job was to stay with her at all times while Carl Mather, his backup, secured the entrance and exit points and patrolled the perimeter of the house.

With his hair, slightly longer than standard for a federal agent, and his slacks and button-down, along with a blazer she knew covered his shoulder holster, he might have passed for college age. A preppy Georgetown law school student, perhaps.

It was a point of contention for him because she knew his buddies in the service called him Baby Face Hunt. Any time someone said it to him he scowled, which usually made her smile. She took enough grief from him on a daily basis that she loved it when he got a taste of payback.

"And now we're in the bathroom. Why?" he said as if still trying to understand why she had led him here.

"I wanted to talk. In private."

"So talk."

Vivian nodded. This was it. Phase Two. She wanted to tell him how much he'd meant to her these past two years. She wanted to tell him how desperately alone she'd been before he came along. Having lost her mother at twelve had been hard, as it would be for any girl that age. But going through that while her remaining single parent was running for the most visible office in the world hadn't been a cakewalk.

Then Joe came into her life to take over her protection going into college and everything changed. Realistically, she understood she was just an assignment to him. His job. But she also knew when she talked, he listened. And he talked to her, too. They ate most of their meals together, knew about each other's day. Each other's lives and families. Each other's goals and dreams.

In the two years they had been together, somehow he'd become her best friend. The person she most wanted to be with in the world.

The man she…loved.

Except saying all that was apparently not going to happen. She wanted to share everything with him, but now that the moment was here, she could barely breathe.

Shit! It was happening again. She couldn't take enough air into her lungs, and then she started to pant.

"Viv," Joe said, moving in and holding on to her shoulders. Forcing her to meet his gaze. "Look at me. Look at me. Easy now. Deep breath. In. Out. Again. In. Out."

After a few moments she was breathing normally. Joe always had that effect on her minor panic attacks. Like he could will them away.

Only now his expression got harder, darker.

"Okay, for real. Talk to me. What's got you upset? Did someone say something to you? Do something?"

Vivian shook her head. This was supposed to be a fun night. A casual party. They were supposed to be talking about their relationship, only now she could see she was worrying him.

"No, nothing like that. It's just…we've known each other for two years…and I… thought…that… Oh, forget Phase Two."

That was when she did it. It was actually pretty easy. Joe still had his hands on her shoulders. All she had to do was press her body against his. She found his mouth with hers and then wrapped her arms around his waist as if she could hold on for dear life.

This was Phase Three. Everything depended on Phase Three.

She could feel his surprise, feel his hands tighten on her shoulders. She broke away from the kiss and he opened his mouth to say something, but it was too late. She was kissing him again, and this time her tongue was in his mouth and she was tasting him.

Vivian Abigail Eleanor Bennett was kissing Joe Hunt, and it was heaven.

Then her back was pressed hard against the locked door of the bathroom and she felt his tongue thrusting against hers. She thought she might have whimpered. Suddenly he was gone and she was empty.

"What the effing hell was that?" he shouted at her.

Still reeling from desire and excitement, it took her a second to process his words. All she could think about was how her mouth felt. It was the only thing on her body she could feel. Hot, swollen, wet.

He tasted…amazing, and all she knew was that she wanted more. Except he was yelling at her.

Wait. Why was he yelling?

"What are you thinking? I'm seven years older than you and a freaking federal agent!"

"But…"

"But nothing!"

Vaguely, Vivian wondered if the people out in the bedroom could hear them. Mortification started to descend on her. This wasn't how it was supposed to go. She knew how he felt about her. She'd just confirmed it with that kiss.

"You idiot! Is this why you brought me

here? To make some half-assed, immature pass? What? Did Daddy's little princess think she was entitled to some screwing? I'm not your damn slave, Viv. You're my freaking work assignment."

"I didn't... I mean... I love you."

He slammed his hand hard against the door next to her ear, and she jumped. In the two years they had been together she'd never seen him like this. Joe was her rock, her stability. Joe was the person who made the fear dissipate. Joe took panic attacks away and made her feel like she could do anything she set her mind to.

He'd been annoyed with her at times, sure, but he never got angry. Never like this.

"You're nothing but a stupid kid. What the hell do you know about love?" he asked softly.

She heard each word. Deep, as if they had penetrated her skin instead of her ears. Somehow her world had just exploded in front of her, and everything she knew to be real was fake.

She turned, fumbled with the lock and ran out of the bathroom.

"Vivian!"

She heard him shout her name, but she

didn't stop. She ran down the steps, push-ing everyone out of her way, oblivious to the stares and whispers that followed her. They were always there, like a soundtrack to her life.

What was the matter with the president's daughter?

Did someone upset the princess?

Then she was out on the sidewalk. Her breaths were shallow and she couldn't get con-trol over them. She needed to calm down. To focus. But the one person who could help her do that was the last person she wanted to see.

Then she heard someone coming up behind her, felt a hand reach around and put some-thing over her mouth. She tried to pull away when it all went dark.

JOE WAS GOING to kill her.

Hopefully, right after he saved her life.

It was the one thought that kept surfacing once Vivian had regained consciousness in the freezing-cold cabin, blindfolded, naked and tied to a chair.

No, it would be okay. Joe would come for her. Yes, he was angry with her. Yes, she knew this was her fault for running away from him, but it wouldn't stop him. Nothing would stop him until he found her.

She tried to bring his face into focus through the fear. Except the only face she saw was the angry version of him. The one who called her a child and an idiot.

She needed the other Joe. The one who made her less afraid. She'd suffer anything to have him here right now, kneeling in front of her and telling her to count her breaths.

Breathe. Just breathe.

That was what she'd been doing, Vivian remembered now. She ran away from Joe, something she would no doubt receive a severe lecture about. She was never supposed to leave his line of sight at an unsecured event. His definition of a party.

Only she had to get away from him. She remembered getting to the sidewalk, struggling for some air and then...

The hand. A hand coming around her face, pressing against her mouth and nose. She hoped she hadn't simply fainted with fear. That her kidnapper had used some kind of drug. Otherwise, that would result in yet another lecture from Joe.

He'd been diligent about teaching her self-defense, an hour almost every day. He would be disheartened to know she hadn't even attempted to fight off her attacker. Hadn't even reached for her panic button.

Nothing.

Yes, The Hand had to have been holding something. Or maybe he knocked her out with a blunt blow to the head. Vivian tried to concentrate on whether she hurt anywhere, but the truth was she couldn't feel a thing.

Except the cold and the brush of the ropes across her shins, stomach and breasts, irritating her bare skin.

She didn't think she'd been raped while she was unconscious. She was a virgin, so she had to believe if The Hand had raped her, she would be sore between her legs. She wasn't. However, as it had gotten colder, numbness took over and she couldn't be certain of anything.

At least he hadn't touched her that way since she woke up. How long had it been?

At least one day. Despite the blindfold, she could tell there was a subtle change in the light in the room. There had to be windows here, letting in the sun. How long she'd been unconscious before that, she had no idea.

Vivian didn't know what was worse—when she was alone like she was now, or when he came to her. Shouting passages from the Bible. Calling her wicked names. Beating her, then crying that he was sorry as he told her how much he loved her.

At least during those moments she was focused. The pain helped to keep the numbness at bay. She also listened for clues in his words, his manner of speech, hoping he might reveal his identity or where he was hiding her.

She'd seen movies like this. Eventually, he was going to have to call her father. She knew Daddy and the Secret Service would be waiting to take the call. When that happened, her father would demand to speak to her to prove she was still alive. She wanted to be able to give him and Joe, who she was sure would be right next to her father, an indication of where she was.

So far she'd only been able to determine they were someplace drafty with no central heat. Her kidnapper had a Southern accent and he knew his Bible really well. The Hand had given nothing else away.

"Vivian! Oh, Vivian! Where are you, slut?"

Her body shuddered at the sound of his

voice. He was back. Somewhere in the house. The panic returned, and she forced herself to take full breaths.

She could hear the creak of the door opening. Felt that she was no longer alone in the room.

"There you are. Right where I left you. That's a good girl. A very good girl."

Her heart started beating against her rib cage like it was trying to get out of her body. Although she found herself almost grateful for the adrenaline rush that warmed her a little.

She attempted again to talk to him. To reason with him.

"My father," she said through chattering teeth, "will pay you whatever you ask."

The Hand laughed, the sound more grating than his Bible verses.

"I don't want your daddy's money, Sugarplum. I want you. I love you. I want you to be with me. Forever. But I need to purify you first. I need you to come to me like a baby comes to her momma. When I know you're clean then we can go away together."

Moving her would mean a chance at escape. "I…think I'm clean now."

She wasn't at all. She'd peed herself twice since being here.

Since she couldn't see beyond the blindfold, she was unprepared for the heavy backhand across her face, followed by a second and a third. Then a solid fist against her left temple made her head spin.

Although she should have expected it by now. He apparently didn't like sass.

You're losing it, Vivian. Get a grip now!

It was Joe's voice in her head. Typical of him to be so harsh with her at a time like this. She would never understand why she had chosen to fall in love with a man as unforgiving as Joe Hunt. Then she actually giggled. Foolish girl. She was a child. What did she know about love?

"You're not clean. You're dirty! Dirty. Evil and dirty. I know because I see it in your eyes and in all those pictures they take of you. I see the dirt, and I want to cry because I know you want to be clean. Don't you, Sugarplum? Don't you want to be clean?"

"I…want…to…be…clean," she stuttered. "Maybe I could have a blanket and wipe myself off."

The Hand connected with her right cheek this time.

Okay, the hitting was starting to piss her off. Although maybe that was a good thing. The anger mixed with her fear might keep her warm a little longer. Which was important because if she died of hypothermia before Joe rescued her, she was sure she'd never hear the end of it.

Wait, she thought hazily, *that didn't make sense*. She tried to shake off the low buzzing in her head. She needed to stay clear. She needed to listen for clues.

"Sugarplum, Sugarplum, I don't *want* to hurt you. I *have* to hurt you because you don't understand. You can't get clean from the outside. You need to get clean from the inside. Do you understand now?"

She let her head fall forward a few times.

"Goooood," The Hand crooned. Then he began to stroke her hair. "You'll see, Sugarplum. This will work. You'll get clean and I will have been the one to save you. Then we can be together. Forever."

She didn't want to ask, but she had to know. "What if... I...don't...get clean?"

A thin point of pressure against the base of

her throat penetrated the numbness. It wasn't a gun. It was too thin. Sharp. A knife.

"Then I'm going to have to *make* you clean. I'm going to have to open you up so I can get the dirt out. Then I will baptize you in your own blood. You'll like that. You will at least be clean for God."

"Oh…kay…" she muttered, losing all sense of what he was saying. She was fading. She felt it. Her body was starting to shut down, and for the first time Vivian considered what might happen if Joe didn't get to her in time.

"I don't want to do it, Sugarplum. I surely don't. God has told me that you are my one and only beloved, and you must sparkle if you are going to be with me. But if I can't get you to sparkle…if I can't make you shine…then I have to kill you, don't you see? I can't let you be with anyone else. Not when you're so dirty. Clean with me or dirty and dead."

"Joe… Joe," she muttered like a mantra over and over again.

"Very slowly, put the knife down and back away from the woman."

Vivian lifted her head at the new voice in the room. She hadn't heard the door over The Hand's talking.

"Joe," she cried out.

"Shut up, Vivian."

Yep, that sounded just like him.

"No!" The Hand cried out in return. "You can't have her! She's a dirty slut, but she's mine. She's mine. She's all mine!"

"This is your last warning. Put the knife down and step away from the chair."

"Never! I love her. I love Sugarplum this much!"

Three successive shots rang out. Vivian felt a heavy weight fall against her body, and then she felt something wet and warm run down her stomach and legs.

The smell of it hit her like a punch in the gut.

Blood.

Then she didn't feel anything anymore.

JOE SAT IN the waiting area of the hospital, his head in his hands.

What did I do? What did I do?

The single question kept rolling over in his head, and he couldn't turn it off. He probably should have been more focused on the events of the last three days. Working with the FBI, identifying Harold McGraw through footage at various public events, tracking down an obscure piece of property in northern Virginia he owned. Only forty miles outside DC.

It had been good work by everyone on the team, and they found her. Alive.

It had been the first time he'd discharged his weapon as an agent, and it had been lethal. Joe didn't care, so why did he keep asking the question?

What did I do? What did I do?

He knew the answer.

I let her go. I let her go. I let her go.

He heard a door open, and then several people were walking down the hospital corridor toward him. Secret Service in front of and behind the president. Joe got up and walked to intercept them. He had to know how she was.

"Sir," Joe began.

The two men in front of the president stepped aside, and Joe noticed how much older Alan Bennett looked today than he had just three days ago. As if he'd aged three years instead.

"Please, sir. If you could tell me how she is. Anything. I'm going crazy waiting for some kind of news."

The look of contempt on the president's face might have made another man back off, but Joe wasn't going anywhere.

STEPHANIE DOYLE   25

Yes, he knew he deserved the older man's rage. Joe had given a full report to the president immediately after Vivian had been taken. He had claimed total responsibility for allowing her to leave his line of sight voluntarily. He hadn't told the full truth, of course. He would never go there. Certainly not with her father.

He'd said only that they had argued and exchanged harsh words. Vivian had been upset and Joe had thought she needed a moment to gather her composure.

Carl, his backup, had been monitoring the back of the house. It had taken Harold McGraw only minutes to knock her out and put her in his van. Drunken college students watched it happen like it was some kind of fraternity prank. So damn easy.

"I've given notice to your superior. You're not on suspension. You're terminated. Effective immediately. Now leave my sight."

Joe dropped his head. "Understood, sir. But if I could just see her…"

That was when he heard it. A shrill scream from behind the door the president had just exited.

"Joe! I need Joe!"

"If I could see her... I might help to calm her panic attacks."

"Jooooe! Joe! Where is he?"

"Good question, Joe. Where were you?" The president didn't wait for an answer and instead closed his eyes. His pain was a tangible presence in the hallway. When he opened them, Joe knew for certain he was never going to see Vivian Bennett again.

"I...failed her. I know. But I can help her now."

"I think you've done enough."

Joe nodded. This man wasn't going to let him pass. "Please, if you just tell me... Mc-Graw, did he...? I mean the rape kit...was it...?"

He couldn't even get the words out, but in what must have been a moment of empathy, the president said, "He didn't rape her."

The breath left Joe's body then, and he thought he actually might pass out. She'd been beaten, psychologically abused, but not sexually assaulted. Her first time wasn't that. It was small comfort, but he had to know.

"Thank you. For that. Now you have to promise me you'll take care of her," Joe begged. "I know you're the president, but you have to be her father now."

"Where's Joe! I want Joe!"

Joe closed his eyes against the anguish in her voice. "You have to promise me. Please… I can't leave her unless I know that."

President Bennett got up in his face. "If you don't leave now, my men will assume you are a credible threat to myself and my family and have you arrested."

Joe dropped his head. He had no choice. He turned and walked down the hallway as fast as he could without running. Not because he was afraid of being arrested but because if he had to listen to the sound of Vivian screaming for him for another second he was pretty sure he was going to lose his mind.

CHAPTER TWO

Present Day

JOE HANDED THE woman in front of him a tissue from a box he kept on his desk at all times for just such an occasion.

"I'm very sorry, Karin. Unfortunately the evidence is pretty conclusive. Your husband is having an affair with his coworker."

He thought it helped for him to say the words out loud. As a private investigator who had shown a number of spouses evidence of adultery, he knew his clients often didn't believe him until he had spoken the words.

Maybe there is a reason you have a photo of him removing her blouse.

Maybe there is a reason his car was parked at a remote area and she was facedown in his lap.

Maybe there is a reason why her tennis appointment every Wednesday is conducted at a small hotel downtown and neither she nor her instructor is ever seen holding rackets.

Joe had heard it all. Which was why he said the words out loud. Only, having to say them to a seven-months-pregnant woman left a more bitter taste in his mouth than usual.

"What do I do?"

"You need to decide that for yourself, but I strongly suggest talking to him first. Be honest. Give him a chance to be honest in return."

Another part of the script. What Joe was really thinking was that she should throw the jerk out on his ass, take half his money, and find someone who would be decent and faithful to her.

He heard voices in the hallway outside his office, and through the beveled glass he could see two tall figures in suits standing just outside. Joe's office was a single room, so when he was meeting with a client, he kept the door locked to prevent interruption.

Karin apparently had heard enough. He handed her a few more tissues, told her he would send his final bill and then walked her out the door.

He wasn't at all surprised to see who was

waiting for him. It had only been a matter of time.

"Hi, Joe," the older man said as he offered his hand.

"Hey, Carl. Long time no see."

Carl nodded grimly. "This is Special Agent Mark Thompson. If you have a few minutes, we would like to talk to you."

Special Agent Thompson was a young fresh-faced man who reminded Joe of himself at that age. The man pulled out and showed his badge to Joe.

"Yeah," Joe said. "I know what they look like."

"Sir, we're here in an official capacity. We think it best to stick to the formalities."

Joe looked at Carl. "Official capacity. Well, this sounds important."

Even as he opened the door and let the two men in, he could feel his heart pounding in his chest.

He sat behind his desk while they took the guest chairs in front of him.

"I don't know if you heard that Ms. Bennett is back in DC. She's opened a new store in town and was recently featured in a local newscast."

Joe nodded once. Of course he knew she was back.

"In the past few months, she's been receiving anonymous notes." Carl took out a laminated piece of paper and set it on his desk. "Does anything about this letter look familiar to you?"

I'm coming for you, Sugarplum.

Block letters, from different print mediums. "No, the letter is not familiar."

His brain was reeling. Someone was threatening Vivian. Someone was calling her Sugarplum. He knew that name. He knew the last time she'd heard it. It had been right before he'd shot Harold McGraw.

Joe's jaw clenched as it finally dawned on him why two members of the Secret Service were here in his office.

"What the hell is this, Carl?"

"Sir, we're looking into anyone who might have been involved in the Bennett kidnapping," Agent Thompson answered. "As a person of interest."

Joe nearly growled. "Carl, you have five seconds to shut this little puppy's mouth and tell me what the hell is going on."

"Sir—" the kid began.

"Thompson. Shut it," Carl snapped. "Sorry, Joe. Direct orders. Vivian told her father about the letters and he asked us to look into it. She's not under SS protection unlike her father. Although currently he only requires a detail when he's out of the country."

"The former president is in China. Shouldn't you be with him?"

Carl frowned. "Never made it onto his detail team."

Right, Joe thought. Because while Carl had for the most part been blameless in "the Bennett kidnapping," as the puppy referred to it, it had still happened on his watch. The president wouldn't have forgotten that. One more thing Joe could claim responsibility for destroying. Carl's career potential.

"So you're investigating the source of these letters."

"She reported the letters to the MPD, but they haven't been able to provide much information. She told her father and…"

"And the federal government is now involved. I get it," Joe said, and he did. Alan Bennett was a commander of men. If he asked for something, he got it. Always. "But seriously, Carl? You have to know I would never…"

"I do. But here is the thing. According to Vivian, she only told one other person Mc-Graw referred to her as Sugarplum."

"Me?"

"No, her therapist."

Joe tried to keep his expression blank, but it wasn't easy. Not when the world knew what McGraw had done to her.

"But it occurred to me that you were there with her in the cabin," Thompson said. "You might have heard McGraw use the name, as well. I communicated that to President Bennett, and he agreed you should be checked out, as well."

Joe almost laughed. Bennett knew damn well Joe had nothing to do with terrorizing Vivian. This visit was just his way of telling Joe to stay clear of her. Which was why Joe hadn't been all that surprised by their arrival. He'd almost expected it since learning she was back in DC.

Ten years was a long time. But not long enough to forget. At least not for President Bennett.

"I can't help you," Joe said finally.

He stood and shook hands with Carl. He ignored the puppy.

Then he decided he'd had a hell of day and needed a drink.

THE DOOR TO the bar opened, and a ray of bright light poured in. For a moment the place seemed to glow, then once more it sank back into its familiar gloominess. Joe could hear someone walking toward him on high-heeled shoes, delicately clicking against the floor. And he knew. He knew it before he turned his head.

"Hi, Joe."

Vivian Abigail Eleanor Bennett. The last time he saw her, her eyes were swollen shut and her lips were parched and split. But now the angry red gash on her forehead had healed. The ugly purple bruises on her face and collarbone had vanished. Although he noticed she had dark circles under her eyes.

She was stunning. As a young woman she had been pretty, made even more so by how little she realized it. Ten years later and she was drop-dead gorgeous. Same blue eyes and long blond hair, but the ten years had only added to her looks.

Her mother had been a Southern Belle

Beauty Queen champion, so it was no surprise where her looks came from. Still, it jolted him.

"May I sit?"

He nodded, unable to find the words after all these years. It was a tie between *I'm so sorry I let you go* and *You ruined my life.*

He couldn't imagine it would be much different for her. Something along the lines of *I shouldn't have kissed you* and *You bastard, how could you let that monster hurt me?*

The bartender approached her and hiked his chin as a signal he was ready for her order. Dom's wasn't a really formal place.

"I'll have what he's having." She smiled.

"I'm having a shot of Jack and a Guinness chaser."

"I'll have a Chardonnay," she said and then placed a bill on the bar, which Dom traded for the glass of wine.

Joe shook his head. It was surreal. He could turn his head and look at her. Talk to her. When for so long she'd been nothing but an image on a screen. For weeks after he'd been fired, he'd watched every second of media coverage he could find, replaying it over and over again so he could see for himself how she was healing. If the bruises were fading. If she was still favoring her right side.

Then, of course, came the interview. The one that was supposed to settle the incident and repair the American psyche. After all, if the president's daughter could be abducted and abused by a monster, then no one in this country was safe.

Then the *other* incident happened. Joe hadn't stuck around to watch that.

Now she was sitting next to him drinking a glass of wine he could tell was foul by the way she winced after every sip.

"What the hell are you doing here, Viv?"

She set the glass aside and turned to face him. Again he was struck by how beautiful she'd become. Or maybe he'd forgotten how pretty she'd been back then because he had always shut down those thoughts.

Mostly.

"I'm sorry about what happened today. I had no idea that Carl would…"

"Question me? Interrogate me? Suspect me?"

She gulped. "Any of those things, I suppose."

Joe shrugged. "Hey, just another day getting my life turned upside down by the Bennetts. Not like that hasn't happened before."

Vivian nodded. "I guess I deserved that."

She didn't deserve any of it, he thought. Yet she deserved all of it, too.

"You ruined my life," he said and laughed. Because she would hear one thing, but he knew it to mean something else entirely.

"I'm sorry," she whispered. Then she laughed, too. "Wow, that felt good. For so long I've thought about how to tell you that. At one point I thought maybe skywriting it over an Orioles' home game. 'Joe. Hunt. I'm. Sorry.' Big block letters so I would know you would see them. It actually feels strange to finally say it."

It would have been easy enough to say she had nothing to be sorry for. It would be easy for him to ask forgiveness for screwing up and letting her get hurt. But they'd both be lying if they forgave each other.

"I did try to fix it. I didn't know you had been fired. I thought you had resigned. Cindy, remember her?"

The agent who should have been on point detail that night instead of him. "Yeah. I remember her."

"She told me what really happened. I went to Daddy, but he didn't want to listen…then I sent a letter to your superior at the time and I explained to him what happened. You deserved your job back."

"That was you," Joe said, remembering the odd call he'd gotten from Tom, his old boss, a few years ago. It had been right after Bennett left office after his second term. Tom determined that Joe hadn't been given a fair hearing. Tom wanted to know if Joe would consider reinstatement under suspension, on condition of a formal review of the incident.

Joe had been too far removed from his old life to think about going back. No, he had his freedom, his business, the life he'd built after his spectacular failure. It wasn't great, but he owned it. Grasping at the past didn't feel like a solution because nothing could be undone.

Things could only begin again.

"I thought you would go back," she said.

"I didn't want it."

"I thought maybe the Colonel…"

"The Colonel was dead by then." So there was no hope of regaining his father's approval. Not that Joe would have wanted it. He could be just as stubborn as his old man.

"I know. I just meant I thought you might do it for him."

Joe looked at her. "How did you know about the Colonel?"

"Your mom," Vivian said as if it were obvious. "You must know we still keep in touch. We're friends on Facebook. I get to see all the grandchildren your siblings are producing. Your nephew Mike looks exactly like you. He's mastered your serious frown."

She was smiling like it was a shared moment between them, but his mind was blown. No, he didn't know she was in touch with his mother this entire time. On Facebook? It was inconceivable.

Did his father know that? Vivian Bennett hadn't been a popular topic in the Hunt household after the kidnapping.

"Why are you here?" he asked again, suddenly irritated. With her, with his mother for not telling him she was talking to Vivian. And that his mother knew how Vivian was doing while he did not. That his mother would have seen pictures of that life on freaking Facebook of all things.

"To apologize for Carl's visit. It must have surprised you to learn I was back in DC."

"I knew you were back," he admitted. "Too many people I know who knew you. They loved telling me, too, like they expected some kind of reaction. You have to love people and their desire to create drama."

Another lie. He had heard she was back, that was true. What she didn't know was that he'd gone to her store in Georgetown. Vivian's Creations. He'd played out a dozen scenarios where he opened the door and walked inside. Said hello.

In the end, he'd left without entering.

It wasn't that he didn't want to see her. It was more like he didn't want to be the one who made the first move. Which was ridiculous. It was entirely possible Vivian never wanted to see him again. He thought maybe it would be better if they met in a Starbucks, or the Metro. Some place where they could run into each other casually.

Except Carl and the puppy showed up before any of that happened. Now she had come to him. Yes, this was much better, he decided, letting go of his irritation. Because he was pretty damn sure she hadn't tracked him down to Dom's to apologize for a few questions from the Secret Service.

"No, Viv, I mean why are you *really* here?"

She squirmed on the stool and then reached to fiddle with her diamond earring, something she did when she got nervous. Only they hadn't been diamonds back in college. Just simple hoops or studs.

It made him wonder how well she was doing with her business that she could afford diamonds. Despite Daddy being loaded, she'd never wanted his money. She used to talk about it all the time, making her own way. Becoming her own woman. Someone who wasn't always in the shadow of her overbearing father.

Joe had pointed out that having Daddy pick up the college tab was a pretty big helping hand. Joe's father certainly wouldn't have paid for any private college. His children had the option of the military or bust.

Still, there was a part of him that couldn't help feeling proud that she'd earned her success.

"You mean why did I come back to DC?" she asked, and he knew she was playing innocent. He let her have a pass. None of this shit between them was easy.

"Yeah. Why now after all these years?"

"Daddy's getting older. You wouldn't know it to look at him, but I realized hiding away on the other side of the country I was missing out on time I could be spending with my father. Suddenly I wasn't afraid to come back anymore."

"Did you have a business out there?"

That made her smile. "Still do," she said, not hiding her pride. "I have some really talented people running it for me, while I get Vivian's Creations off the ground here. I'm a chain now. Who would have ever have thought I might actually do something productive?"

"Me. I did."

She met his eyes and then focused on the wineglass instead and nodded. "Yeah, you did. Always giving me pep talks."

"I knew what it was like to have a father like yours. Always feeling like you never measured up. I felt I needed to offset that."

"Yes, but my father loves me, too."

Joe couldn't say what the Colonel had felt for him. Love? If it was, it was fleeting after Joe had failed the nation.

"Don't be mad."

Joe's lips twitched. Vivian always told him

that when she knew whatever she was going to say next would make him mad.

"What?"

"I went to him."

"Who?"

"The Colonel. I wrote a letter to your mother. I thought it was important that your family know the truth…"

"Hell, Vivian. Are you serious? What the hell did you say?"

"That you weren't to blame. That we got into a fight and I ran away from you. That it was my fault. I didn't mention…the other thing."

The kiss. A kiss he hadn't forgotten in ten years.

Joe was still trying to process why she thought the truth exonerated him.

"Your mom asked me to come and talk to him. To try to make him understand. I think she was heartsick about how he'd treated you. Plus, she probably missed having you around. I said everything I could, but he never looked at me once. When I ran out of words, he said thank you and left the room."

One more thing to be angry with that bastard over, being a jerk to Vivian.

"I could have told you what his reaction would be."

"Maybe. But you weren't there."

The jab hurt, and he looked at her to see if she'd said it intentionally. Reminding him of his many sins. Leaving Vivian at the hospital and never looking back.

Sometimes he could still hear her screaming in that broken voice.

Where is he?

So many sins. How could she possibly forgive them all?

One more time. "Why are you here, Viv?"

"I'm scared," she admitted. "Not really something new for me, but with these notes…"

It wasn't the answer he wanted, but at least she wasn't lying. He could feel her fear in her tight, shallow breaths.

"Carl's going to handle it. He'll find whoever did this. Some nutjob who saw you on the news and now wants his fifteen minutes."

She shook her head. "It's not enough. I have a lot on my plate starting this new business, rebuilding my life here in DC. I can't do that looking over my shoulder everywhere I go. I want to feel safe. I need to feel safe.

Which is why I'm here. I want to hire you to protect me."

Now that, Joe thought, was irony. Then he burst out laughing.

CHAPTER THREE

IT WASN'T EXACTLY the reaction she expected. She waited until he had calmed down, but noted that there were actual tears in his eyes. She didn't think she'd ever seen him laugh so hard.

"It's not that funny."

"Yes. It is. You want me, of all people, to protect you?"

Vivian took a deep breath. She'd known coming here wouldn't be easy, but she'd also known he was her best option and her first choice.

"I'm no longer entitled to Secret Service protection, and I wouldn't want that anyway. I could hire another investigator, but that person wouldn't know me and wouldn't really understand the situation like you do."

And the last time she had felt truly safe in her life was when Joe had been watching over her. She wanted that again. She was willing to sacrifice her pride to get it. It wasn't a question that he could have forgiven her. A foolish stunt by a twenty-year-old girl who thought she was madly in love…

You were *madly in love*.

Regardless, she thought, her feelings had cost him his job, his future and his relationship with his father. Not to mention what that did to the rest of his family. Vivian considered what might happen when she saw him again.

That he might yell, or worse tell her to get lost in that scary soft tone he always used when he was superangry.

Laughing was unexpected.

Then suddenly he stopped. "You do recall what happened the last time you were under my protection?"

Yes, because she'd been stupid. Vivian shrugged. "I'm guessing you won't make that mistake again. You were the best at what you did, Joe. I know that, even if no one else does."

He huffed. "You don't know anything about me anymore."

Yes, it had been ten years, but back when they had been together, she had known Joe Hunt.

"I hear that Hunt Investigations has a sound

reputation and that you come highly recom-
mended. I did some research before I made
the decision to find you."

She couldn't read his expression. Maybe
pride? Then he closed it down. "Yeah, I'm
aces at catching cheating spouses in the act.
Just ask anyone. No marriage is safe when Joe
Hunt is on the trail."

"Surely you must work other cases."

He stared at her hard for a moment and then
shook his head. "I don't think this is a good
idea. For either of us. Find someone else."

"There is no one else!" Vivian blurted out.
She felt it. She was losing the battle. Losing
him. The thought of that, aftcr shc'd had to
summon all her courage to see him again, was
unthinkable. "No one I trust. No one who can
take away the constant feeling that I'm being
watched…"

Her breathing got shallow, and she could
feel the panting begin, the panic escalating.

Not in front of him. Not in front of him.

"Look at me, Viv. Eyes on me."

Helpless to resist, she met his eyes and felt
his hands on her shoulders to hold her steady.

"Deep breath." He breathed it in with her.
"Another one. Again."

She repeated the effort until her breathing regulated. Her face, though, was flush with humiliation. She'd hated that lack of control.

"Still get them?"

"Not as much," she said tightly. In fact she hadn't had so much as a hiccup in years. Not until she got the first note. Then it all came flooding back.

"It's the letters. They're upsetting. The name... No one knew that name, Joe. It's not possible he's..."

"He's dead."

Vivian nodded. Intellectually she knew that. Three sharp blasts, then the feeling of his blood spilling out of his body and onto her legs. Warming her after she'd been so cold.

She shuddered and tried to focus on the facts. Joe knew he was dead because Joe had killed him.

"Sugarplum," she muttered. "To this day I can't even look at a plum in the grocery store. Pathetic I realize, but a fact."

"Are you sure you never used the name with anyone?" he asked. "Told some reporter at some time? It would have been easy to let it slip. You were constantly being hounded for comments."

Vivian considered it, but no, it wasn't possible. She hadn't been able to say the name at all. When trying to give the federal agents as much detail about the time spent as his prisoner, even thinking the name caused her to shut down completely.

It wasn't until she'd started therapy with Nicholas that she'd finally been able to recount more of the details of her kidnapping. Something he assured her she needed to do to put it behind her.

But Nicholas wasn't someone she necessarily wanted to remember, either. She certainly didn't want to discuss him with Joe. For now she didn't see the point. Carl and his agents were going to investigate the origin of the letters. Joe was simply the body man she needed to watch her back.

The less said about her time with Nicholas, the better for both of them. Only, there was the small matter of Joe not wanting to take the job.

"I know this is strange," she began. "For both of us. I know I'm probably the last person you ever wanted to see again, and now I'm asking you for something, as well. You can say no if you hate me that much. It's okay for you to walk away. But if any part of you remembers who we used to be before it all happened, then I'm asking as your old friend to help me."

He lifted the remaining glass of whiskey and swallowed it in one gulp.

"Okay. You win. Let's go."

"Where are we going?"

"You remember how it works, Viv? Where you go I go. Which means I've got to check out your place."

Right, Vivian thought. She was taking Joe back to her place.

She could handle that. At least she hoped she could.

"WHERE'S YOUR BED?"

They were back at her apartment and Joe was moving from room to room. Finally he joined her in the kitchen, and Vivian tried to think straight.

It was hard when part of her wanted to pinch herself. It was surreal to her that he was actually here with her now. Not a dream. Not a memory.

He was certainly older. Some gray was smattered throughout his dark brown hair. A beard grew tight along his jaw. Back in the day the other agents had called him Baby Face Hunt, much to his chagrin. No one could say that now.

Of course, he was still handsome. She'd never expected that to change, and she didn't think she would ever look at Joe Hunt and think him not handsome. His eyes were still the same. Deep, dark brown and intense. Although now there were lines around the edges, like rings in a tree marking the years of his life.

And when he asked her where her bed was, she felt a pang.

Not good.

A series of thoughts ran through her head. Did he want to take her to bed? Would she let him? Were they finally going to do what she'd felt had been destined for them all those years ago? Was this the thing they could do that would finally close the door on their past and let her move on with her life?

"It's not an invitation. Just a question," he elaborated.

Or maybe he just wanted to know where her bed was.

Mentally, Vivian scolded herself. She knew better than to indulge those feelings.

Adolescent crush. Hero worship. Fantasy-based infatuation. These were the terms Nicholas had used to describe her feelings toward Joe. Which in many ways helped. If he hadn't been that important to her, then it wouldn't have hurt as much that he left her when she needed him most.

Except he had been. Important. And it had hurt.

Back then.

"I don't have a bed."

"From what I can tell, this is a one-bedroom apartment. That room back there is supposed to be the bedroom. All you've got in there is some fancy couch, a nightstand and a walk-in closet."

"It's a chaise lounge," she corrected him.

"Whatever. Where do you sleep?"

"I don't sleep much," Vivian answered. She didn't want to talk about it. She didn't want him to see the ripple effects of the kidnapping in her life. She wanted him to see how much she'd changed and grown. Not how much she was still broken.

Half answers had never been enough for

him, though, and she could see he was waiting for more.

Vivian shrugged. "I have insomnia."

"Even insomniacs sleep some of the time."

"I sleep some, yes. On the couch here. In that leather recliner behind you. Sometimes on the chaise. Whenever my body needs it. You're not supposed to lie in a bed and not sleep. It develops bad patterns. You begin to associate the bed with not sleeping. I didn't want to develop any long-term issues with beds in general. Sooner or later I'm going to get over this. Then I'll need one. For now, no bed."

"You never used to have a problem sleeping."

Vivian gave him a look that implied he was being thick.

He nodded. "You haven't slept in ten years? You look remarkably well, considering."

"I sleep. I just don't sleep in a bed."

"Must be hell on your boyfriends," he commented, walking past her toward a wall she had filled with framed pictures of herself and her father. She'd once stood next to dignitaries, presidents, congressmen and a queen. She wondered if Joe remembered those times. He'd been at most of those occasions with her.

Then he looked over his shoulder at her with a shitty little grin. "Then again, I guess shrinks don't have a problem doing it on a couch."

Wow. A direct hit. She'd been waiting for it. It had to come up sometime. His disdain over what had happened with Nicholas. It was why she'd avoided mentioning his name back at the bar.

Still, she hadn't been prepared for how much it would hurt. Hadn't been prepared for him to hurt her so intentionally.

Something he would do only if he hated her.

This had been a mistake, she thought. A mistake to come to him for help. She thought he could make her feel safe. He thought she had ruined his life. Of course he would want to hurt her, punish her.

"You're right, Joe," Vivian said calmly. "What a funny joke."

His expression changed. Almost as if he regretted the words, but it was too late. Now she knew the truth. He really did hate her, which meant she was never going to feel safe with him.

"Vivian…"

"This isn't going to work."

He shoved his hands in his pockets and looked away from her. "I didn't mean… I was just…"

"Being an ass? What? You thought reminding me about my scandal would make me laugh?"

If it was possible, Nicholas Rossi had been a bigger mistake than running away from Joe that night.

"Just like that, then? You said you needed me and now I'm expendable."

"I can't… I can't…" She paused and took a deep breath, then another. She was not a weak person, she told herself firmly. She was not. "I can't do this, Joe. I can't fight whoever is trying to scare me and you, too. When I found you, I thought I would find…"

Safety and peace. What she'd had before with him before it all shattered. It had been a fool's errand. A person couldn't go back.

"Find what?" he asked.

Vivian shook her head. "It doesn't matter. I was wrong. I'm sorry for taking you away from your afternoon bender. You can bill me for your time."

"What about your phantom stalker?"

She smirked. "Phantom? So you don't think he's real? Well, then I guess I'm as safe as I can be."

"I didn't say that. The letters are real."

"They are, but who is to say who sent them? Maybe I sent them to myself. We both know I'm not exactly stable," she said, a note of hysteria in her rising tone. "Heck, I used to see a shrink, right? Of course, after I seduced him, our sessions were more physical than mental. Not really much time for talking or working out your emotional issues when you're committing adultery!"

"Calm down, Vivian."

A typical Joe Hunt command delivered with simplicity and authority. There was never an order he barked that she didn't obey. Sometimes she used to put up a good fight, but in the end she always capitulated. That was then.

"No, I won't calm down!"

He moved toward her, and she knew what he would do. Grab her shoulders, make her look him in the eyes, breathe with her. And she didn't want that again. She didn't want to remember he could soothe her so easily.

Why had she done this? Why had she

opened herself up to all of this again? She
never should have gone looking for him.

"No," she said, backing away from him. "I
don't have to do what you say anymore. Leave.
Your services are no longer required."

For a moment he said nothing, but he didn't
move. She thought he might try to convince
her she needed him. He didn't.

"Whatever you say. You're the boss. See
you around, Viv."

He went out the front door and closed it
slowly behind him.

He'd really left.

Immediately, the atmosphere in her apartment changed from one of comfort and safety
to one of emptiness. She was alone again, and
she didn't know if she could bear it.

*You were alone before. You've been han-
dling this on your own for weeks.*

Yes, but it had been horrible. Sleep, which
was such a valuable commodity to her anyway, had completely eluded her. She was
jumpy and agitated and...

She made bad decisions.

Decisions like finding Joe. Thinking there
could be some resolution to their past.

Thinking that...

Go get him. Tell him you need him.

Another bad idea. Only it was getting harder and harder to tell which ideas were good and which were bad.

If she went after him, she would be humiliated.

But she would have him and he would protect her. This she knew for certain.

Except part of the reason she wanted to see him again was to prove to him she had grown up. She was supposed to be an independent, self-confident and mature woman. The fact that on most days she still felt like a scared little girl didn't matter.

Only the illusion counted. If she went running after him and begged him to come back, he would know she hadn't changed much in the last ten years. He would see her now as everyone had seen her back then. Needy. Clinging.

If that happened, he would never fall in love with her.

Suddenly Vivian wanted to scream. She wanted to smash everything in her apartment just to hear the sound of it splintering apart. She wanted to see physical evidence of what she felt inside.

Why him?

After the scandal with Nicholas had erupted, Vivian had left DC in shame and humiliation. She found a job and a life in Seattle. Then she found a new therapist, Susan, who had actually helped her work through her issues.

She'd begun to understand her dependence on Joe. Vivian had lost her mother at twelve. The woman who had been the center of her universe. Her father had been governor of Virginia at the time. A busy man with a busy schedule, he'd given Vivian every minute he could, but it hadn't been close to what she'd had with her mother. Not enough of what she'd needed.

Her father would be heartsick to know what it had done to her every time he left her for work. Every trip he'd needed to take. Every event he'd needed to attend, leaving her alone at night.

The horrible, overwhelming fear that when he left, he might never come back. Like her mother.

Vivian used to think that aside from her panic attacks, she'd conquered her fear fairly well.

It wasn't until she'd met Joe that she understood she'd only been controlling it. Because it wasn't until she had met him, the fear finally went away.

Her appointed bodyguard. Her very own security net. It had seemed crazy to her. Until the first time she'd tried to ditch him and couldn't. They were at some pizza place not far from the White House. She wasn't sure what had made her do it, but she'd tried to leave through the back door. Maybe to test him. Maybe to tease him. She hadn't gotten ten feet before he was behind her on the sidewalk.

He didn't scold her. He didn't lecture her on the importance of her security. He simply took her back to the restaurant.

That was when she knew. He was never going to let her get into trouble. He would never leave her side.

All reasons why a girl who had lived in fear until that moment would find herself falling in love.

Adolescent crush. Hero worship. Fantasy-based infatuation.

Nicholas had made it seem that what she'd felt for Joe wasn't real. Then, of course, he'd begun to explain to her what was real.

Vivian dropped her face into her hands, the shame and humiliation of how easily she'd been manipulated washing over her like a wave that never stopped coming. She could move past it, she could not let it affect her life, but she could never forget how gullible she'd been.

Susan had helped her deal with that, as well. She'd called out Nicholas for being an abusive monster, preying on a victim when she was at her weakest. That was true, but Vivian had to be honest with herself. She'd let Nicholas seduce her, she'd let him screw her. She'd done it to hurt Joe.

Because Joe had left her.

Eventually, she forgave herself. For everything. Susan had helped her to understand emotions more clearly. If you loved, you loved. If you hated, you hated. If you were afraid, you were afraid, and if you were sad, you were sad. Pretending to feel something else when the other feelings were in charge was a quick way to an ulcer.

So Vivian let herself be sad. She let herself cry because Joe was gone, even though she had told him to leave. Finally she picked herself up, dried her tears and thought about what came next.

She would start looking for another investigator in the morning. Perhaps a woman would be a better option. At least it was a plan.

Changing into some flannel pajamas, Vivian set her cell on the nightstand so it was close at hand. Then she reclined on the chaise lounge as the strain of the day caught up with her.

She hadn't slept at all last night, and she was exhausted. Concentrating on taking deep, slow, even breaths, Vivian felt herself drift off. The sound of her home phone ringing from the other room penetrated, but she had no intention of risking what might be actual sleep to answer it.

Whoever it was could leave a message.

CHAPTER FOUR

"HAIL TO THE CHIEF."

The song broke through her sleep. Vivian lifted her head and reached for her cell phone on the nightstand. It was just after one in the morning. Only her father would think to call her at this time of night, and the ringtone proved it.

"Hi, Daddy."

"Oh, baby, were you actually sleeping and I woke you up? You're never asleep at this hour."

It was true. If she did manage to get a couple of hours in, it was usually between four and seven. Somehow, knowing dawn was approaching made it easier to sleep.

"I know, but don't be upset." Vivian looked at the time again and considered how long she'd been out. "I had four solid hours. That's a lot for me. What's up? How are the China negotiations?"

"They would be going a lot better if everyone in the room simply listened to me."

Vivian smiled as she sat up. "There's a surprise. Alan Bennett thinks he knows what's best for everyone."

"I can't help it if it's true. But I didn't call for that. I want an update on the letter situation. I'm not happy they assigned Mather to review your case. He is incompetent. I've been thinking we should approach this from a different angle. Have someone privately look into the matter."

Vivian almost chuckled. Great minds did think alike. Although she doubted her father would have approved her choice for bodyguard/investigator. All Vivian had to do was mention Joe's name and her father would immediately look like he needed to hit something.

Another reason why letting Joe go was probably a smart idea. She couldn't imagine her father would ever accept him as part of her life. Any part.

"I've considered that, too, Daddy. I'll start researching investigators tomorrow. See if I can find someone I'm comfortable with."

Because that had been the plan, right? Certainly not to go groveling back to Joe. She had her pride, and he'd insulted her. That was way more important than her peace of mind. And her father didn't like him, and…

And when he'd asked where her bed was, she'd imagined something happening between them, and that was more dangerous to her peace of mind than her stalker.

"Okay. I want a list of names next time I call. I'll have them properly vetted. In the meantime, I'm going to talk to the director of the service and see if I can't get him to assign someone more qualified than Mather to investigate."

Mather was how her father referred to Carl after the kidnapping. Carl hadn't shouldered anywhere close to the blame Joe had, but her father's opinion of the man had lowered significantly. Despite trying to explain to her father for years that Carl had nothing to do with her kidnapping, she'd never been able to convince him.

Vivian sometimes wondered who had it worse. Joe for losing his job, or Carl for keeping his but forever being known in the agency to his superiors as *That Carl*. At least Joe had gone on to have something for himself, with no one to answer to.

She wondered if her father would even mention that Carl had seen Joe today. Had questioned him in a formal capacity as a person of interest. Doubtful, since he probably knew it would upset her and he wouldn't want to have that fight. Not over Joe. Not again, when they hadn't had it in so many years.

"I'll get some names and figure out what to do from here," she said. "You worry about saving the world and making it a better place for mankind."

"I can multitask. I'll be back in a few days for Christmas. Speaking of which, there is an event at the end of this week I would like you to attend with me. A fund-raiser for underprivileged children in DC. The president will be in attendance and he's asked me to come."

Vivian was about to agree.

"Jefferson will be there, as well," her father added before she could reply.

Right. Jefferson Caldwell, junior congressman from northern Virginia's district ten. He was handsome, he was charming, but most important he was single and looking for a politically suitable wife.

Despite her scandal, Vivian fit the bill of a suitable political wife with the appropriate political pedigree. She'd met Jefferson on a handful of occasions, all arranged by her father. He'd seemed nice and considerate, but she hadn't felt any spark. Nothing like what she'd felt upon seeing Joe again. The instant attraction. The need to touch any part of him so she was connected to him. The desire to hear him speak, the comfort of having him listen.

There had been a few other men in her life in the last ten years. Nice men. Kind men, other than Nicholas.

One she had liked very much, but as soon as he'd started to hint at marriage she'd called it off, knowing instinctively that wasn't what she wanted from him. Companionship, yes. Commitment, no.

Adolescent crush. Hero worship. Fantasy-based infatuation.

Or love.

It didn't matter what anyone called it, Vivian could only speak to how it felt. Maybe now that she'd seen him again, had said what she'd wanted to say to him, it would start to fade.

Their relationship ten years ago had ended

with an abrupt separation. Because of that, she'd never been able to move beyond those feelings. There had been no resolution to them. Now there was. She'd said she was sorry. He'd said she ruined his life.

Then he'd hurt her. Intentionally. Spitefully.

Now they were over for good. Which meant she had to consider what she wanted her future to be. She wanted love, a husband, children.

None of that was going to happen with Joe Hunt.

"It will be lovely to see him again," Vivian said after a beat. Maybe it would be. For the first time she might be able to look at a man and not compare him with Joe. Accept him at face value for who he was.

"Excellent. Then it's a plan. I love you, sweetie."

"Love you, too, Daddy."

"Try to get some more sleep—that's an order."

Vivian smiled. "Yes, sir."

Although even as she disconnected the call she knew it wasn't going to happen. Her brain was fully awake and she actually felt refreshed. As if her sleep had been deep and steady where usually she tossed and turned and slept in short bursts.

Leaving her bedroom, she headed into the kitchen to scrounge for some food. A plan of hot chocolate and a late-night movie was already starting to form. Vivian stopped, though, when she saw the blinking light on her home phone.

Few people called her on her home phone, as her friends and employees all had her cell.

The automated voice told her she had two new messages. *Wow*, she thought. She'd been so out of it she hadn't even heard it ring the second time. Actual sound sleep.

"Vivian, this is Jefferson. I had hoped to catch you at home."

See, she told herself, *he sounds perfectly normal*. A deep voice with a hint of a Southern accent. There was no reason not to find this man attractive. Except when he'd asked for her phone number, she had purposely given him only her house number, not the cell she always had with her. There was always a sense of distance. Susan used to call these behaviors her barriers. Vivian had always been inclined to build them around herself. The kidnapping had only made that worse.

"I would like to extend you an invitation to a Christmas fund-raising event. I'm sure your father will be there, too, but...well, I would like you to come as my date. The three of us, of course, can sit together."

"Of course we can sit together. Otherwise you lose the chance at a photo-op," she muttered, then immediately winced. She was supposed to be keeping an open mind. It was just that she couldn't help but feel as if Jefferson's interest in her had more to do with her name than her.

It had been the way he'd casually brought up the scandal when they had first met. How she had been a victim. Vulnerable after having survived such a horrific event. Nicholas Rossi had been the villain and should have been treated by the country as such.

The American people must realize that now in hindsight. That was what Jefferson had said.

As if the American people cared at all about a ten-year-old affair, no matter whom she was.

The former president's grown daughter was of no interest to the American people. However, as the wife of an up-and-coming congressman, that could change. Suddenly the name *Bennett* would be back in the political spotlight.

Spin.

His words had felt like spin to her, as if he were already spinning how he would handle any questions related to her very public affair with Nicholas.

Vivian had left DC to stop the spinning.

"Please call me..."

She hit the number to end and save the message, cutting Jefferson off in midsentence. She didn't have the strength to deal with him yet, so the best thing she could do was put him off. Tomorrow she would play the message again and see if the sound of his voice didn't make her cringe, make her think of reporters, cameras and fake smiles. Everything politics was and everything she was not. For now she had to admit she was a little oversensitive.

"Second message."

At first there was nothing. Possibly a hang-up or a wrong number. Then the buzz of a conversation played as if on speaker and Vivian could hear people in the background.

"Why did he do it? Can you tell us that?"

"No. I don't know why he did it. He said he wanted to make me clean. He said he loved me."

"Do you think he loved you?"

"I think he was crazy."

For a moment Vivian didn't understand what she was hearing. It was her voice on the phone. Her voice and Katy Thurman's, the CBS correspondent.

This was the interview. The only interview she'd done after the kidnapping. The one her father had insisted she do, to give the country closure. She'd considered it torture having to share publicly everything she had lived through, because it meant living through it again. Only this time with people watching. As if they could actually see her naked and tied to a chair. Bloody and bruised. No one ever wanted to be that vulnerable. Certainly not her.

But she hadn't been able to say no to her father when he was telling her it was something the American people needed from her.

"How do I ask this without sounding like

*a monster? Is there a part of you that is re-
lieved he was killed? That you don't have to
suffer through a trial where you would have
to confront him every day?"*

*"I'm just glad I'll never have to hear his
voice again."*

There was a pause. Long enough that Vivian might have thought to delete the message
if she hadn't been focused on trying to breathe
past the panic that had gripped her chest. Then
she heard it. It was faint and distant, not as
loud as the replay of the interview had been.
But she definitely heard it.

"Sugarplum. I love you."

This time the surge of fear propelled her
into action. She pulled the phone off the counter. The plug flew out of the socket and the
light on the handset dimmed. She stood there
with it in her hands as if it were a snake ready
to bite her. She considered tossing it in the
trash but realized it didn't make a difference
what she did with it.

She'd gotten the message.

McGraw was still alive. He had to be. It
was the only explanation—that was his voice.
Maybe Joe only thought he had killed him.

Maybe McGraw had been in a coma all this time and had just woken up.

Vivian giggled in a near-hysterical state. She was starting to sound like a writer for a soap opera. McGraw was dead. Closing her eyes, she tried to remember that night. It wasn't a place she often went back to. Her memories were hazy and disjointed. Like clips of a movie she'd never seen from beginning to end.

She was cold. So cold. McGraw was screaming. At her and at Joe.

Shots. Then the sound of Joe's voice.

"You're going to be okay."

"Joe?"

"I'm here, baby. Everything's going to be okay."

"I'm so cold."

Vaguely, she recalled Joe carrying her outside the room where she'd been held. He'd set her down on a chair and kneeled in front of her.

"I'm naked."

"Shh. Shh."

"I don't want you to see me this way."

"It's okay, baby. You're safe with me. Will someone get me a damn blanket!"

"I don't want you to see me this way. Please, Joe. Help me."

At her plea, he'd taken off his Secret Service–issued windbreaker and pulled it over her head. She remembered thinking she wanted to crawl inside it and never come out.

There had been agents all around her barking orders. Everything so loud and chaotic it was hard to focus. Until she understood that if she was sitting with Joe, it meant *The Hand* was dead. She'd wanted to see the body. She remembered needing to be sure.

She'd gotten up and run back into the room before Joe could stop her. FBI agents were standing over the body, and she shoved one from behind to move him out of way.

Then she saw him. Harold McGraw. On the floor at her feet. The knife he'd pricked her with for days an inch or two from his hands. Blood pooled out from underneath him and he didn't move. He never moved. Then Joe was lifting her again, and carrying her out of the room, his arms secured tightly around her.

"Don't look."

"I need to see. I need to know."

"It's over. Everything is going to be okay now. I promise."

"He's really dead?"

"He's dead."

Over his shoulder she'd watched McGraw the whole time as Joe carried her back out of the cabin, waiting to see if he would get up, waiting to see if he would come after her.

He never moved. Not an inch.

He was dead.

Vivian blinked away the memories. Because now she had to question all of it. Her memories, the sound of the gunshots. What if McGraw wasn't dead? The only person she knew to tell was the person who was supposed to have killed him.

Vivian bolted into action. She ran back to her room and pulled on an old pair of jeans, a sweater and some boots. Dashing toward her front door, she noticed the clock in the kitchen and remembered it was the middle of the night.

It didn't matter. She had proof. She had a message with his voice on it. She couldn't have made that up. Joe needed to hear it. He needed to tell her she was wrong and it wasn't McGraw's voice because he was dead. Because Joe had killed him.

Grabbing her coat and purse, she opened

the door and sprinted out into the hallway. Only she didn't get very far. Someone was sitting outside her door, waiting for her.

The feel of a hand wrapping around her ankle paralyzed her at first. Then she began to scream.

CHAPTER FIVE

JOE SAT IN the hallway and leaned back against the wall, preparing for what was going to be a long, uncomfortable night. He took out his phone and stared at it, wondering if there was an app that might keep his mind occupied for the next several hours. He knew there wasn't. Instead he would have all this time to think.

About Vivian.

About the letters.

About Vivian.

Why had he made that comment about the shrink? Joe was nothing if he wasn't honest with himself. She had accused him of wanting to hurt her, but that wasn't it. No, he'd wanted to see her reaction. To assure himself she hadn't actually loved the asshole.

He'd been in Texas when the story broke and watched along with everyone else while Nicholas's wife had called out Vivian publicly as some kind of seductress. That her husband, who had been trying to help the young woman recover, had been made a victim by her sexual aggression.

It was laughable and disgusting.

Only, Vivian didn't deny it. And her father wouldn't defend her. "No comment" was President Bennett's only response to every question fired at him accompanied with a look of grave disappointment.

Joe had been sick with rage. At her father for not calling the bastard out for what he was: a predator. At Nicholas Rossi, who had been twice her age and should have been trying to help her instead of nail her.

At Vivian, for allowing herself to be a victim.

Because there was no other way to describe what had happened to her. She'd been vulnerable, recently traumatized and she'd just lost her best friend. Joe knew that because he'd lost his, too.

Nicholas Rossi should have been shot in the balls.

So why had he taunted her with it? He feared it had a lot to do with simple jealousy. Regardless of the circumstances, and how much time had passed, for a short while she'd belonged to Nicholas, and it left a bad taste in Joe's mouth.

Besides, a little snarkiness would help to keep her at a distance emotionally. Something he knew he was going to need to keep his head clear regarding her.

He snorted. Some distance. He was sitting next to her apartment door because he couldn't not.

When she'd fired him, he'd left. Left and hadn't looked back. The smartest course of action was to get as far away from Vivian Bennett as he could. Intellectually, he knew that.

He'd gotten on the Metro and made it three stops before he got off and took the Green Line back. Then he'd loitered in the lobby for a while. Assessed the building for access points. Decided there were too many ways to get inside than he could monitor, and finally parked himself in the hallway next to her apartment door.

It was a small building. Only four apartments per floor. By the time he made it upstairs, it was late and her neighbors weren't coming and going. Most likely all were tucked in their beds. No one was there to see him and wonder why a strange man was sitting in the hallway.

It was a simple place in the northwest part of the city, not too fancy. Something the owner of an interior design shop might be able to afford. Which meant she'd stuck to her commitment to not live off her father's money. Something he used to goad her about all the time.

Because he'd been a hard-ass back then just like he was now. Or maybe just hard on her. Always so hard on her.

Then the door to her apartment sprang open and she came flying out into the hallway. Thinking only to stop her, he grabbed her ankle. Her scream was nearly ear-piercing.

"Will you be quiet! You're going to wake up the whole damn building," Joe grumbled even as he got to his feet.

"You didn't leave me," she whispered. "You didn't go."

She was looking at him in that way she used to. Like she'd been in pain and he was the thing that made the pain go away. He didn't deserve that look from her anymore.

Moving past her, Joe made his way inside her apartment, and Vivian followed. He heard the door close behind him and thought about how he was going to answer her questions.

"What are you doing here?" she asked. "Why didn't you leave?"

"I need some coffee. Not that your screeching at the top of your lungs didn't do a hell of a job waking me up."

Avoidance, he thought. Not a bad play.

She put her purse and coat down and made her way to the kitchen. Mechanically, she scooped out the coffee, filled the pot and got two mugs out.

Joe wandered over to the recliner and took a seat.

"Wow, this is good stuff. I feel like I could sink in here and never get up," he commented as he pushed himself more firmly into the leather chair.

"That's the idea." she said after a few minutes as she returned with a mug in her hand.

He took the coffee and sipped. Cream and heavy on the sugar. Just as he liked it. She remembered even that.

"I wanted something really comfortable, or more accurately *comforting*," she said as if it was the most normal conversation for them to be having right now.

"It's not the typical piece of furniture you would find in a woman's apartment."

She raised her eyebrows at that. "You were expecting ribbons and bows?"

"And flowers. Lots of flowers," Joe added. "I mean you're a decorator, right?"

Vivian huffed. "Decorating means you have good taste in a number of styles. I can do flowers for those who want them. I don't prefer them. For myself, I choose furniture and accessories in interesting shapes, colors and materials. The leather in the chair you're sitting in is supple and the shape is elegant. It fits very well in that space."

"I guess." He shrugged. He couldn't say what the aesthetic value of the chair was, he just knew it felt good. Joe glanced up from his coffee. The color had returned to her cheeks during her little diatribe. Her breathing had returned to normal. He figured she was over the worst of whatever panic had sent her running out of her apartment in the middle of the night.

"Better?" he asked.

Slowly, she nodded. Her eyes met his in recognition of what he had just done to first distract her, and then calm her down. "Thank you."

"Okay, now why don't you tell me what happened to send you running at two in the morning." And to whom?

"Why don't you tell me what you were doing outside my door first?"

He would eventually, but he wanted his answers first. So he sat and sipped his coffee in silence, knowing Vivian would try to hold out against him but would eventually capitulate. She always did.

He waited while she made a show of being willful. Walking over to the couch, she sat and said nothing. In the end, she just didn't have the patience he did.

"All right," she snapped. "I got a voice message. On my home phone."

Joe looked over to the counter where she'd unplugged the phone from the wall. "From who?"

"He didn't say," she answered. "Sort of takes the fear and panic out of the situation when you know who is terrorizing you. Much more sinister this way. But there was a voice at the end of the message. A voice I recognized. I was coming to find you so you could listen to it."

Him. She'd been running to him.

"You found me."

Vivian got up off the couch and went into the other room. When she came back she was dialing a number on her cell.

She handed him the phone and he listened as the recorded voice said there were two saved messages.

"Jefferson?" Joe asked. "You're kidding me with that name, right?"

"Forget him. Just listen."

Next came the interview excerpt.

"That's from…"

"I know what it is," he said, cutting her off. He didn't need to be reminded he was listening to her interview. He remembered every word. For the most part she had talked about the experience and what it had been like. She also talked about how she had run away from her government protection. How she'd been careless, which was why it happened in the first place. Trying to exonerate him, he supposed.

A noble effort that failed—with his father, her father and the people of the United States. None of whom had been nearly as forgiving as she had been. But then he never really believed she had forgiven him. How could she?

He heard the pause, then the third voice.

Sugarplum. I love you.

"It's him. I know it. You're going to say it's been ten years and my memory might be playing tricks on me, but…"

"He's dead, Viv."

"Yes, but that's his voice. I'm not wrong," she insisted. "I may be scared out of my mind, but I haven't lost it yet. It's him."

"I shot him. Three times in the chest. You saw the body. He's dead."

BANG. BANG. BANG.

Vivian remembered the sound of those shots so vividly. She remembered thinking how loud they were. How she was too near something that could kill her.

Even though she'd been in close proximity to a man who could have killed her at any point in the three days he held her.

Joe was replaying the message after turning up the volume on her phone.

She moved away from him, not wanting to listen to it one more time. Instead she stared out the window that led to the street below. Was someone out there? Watching her? Waiting to see how she would react to the message?

The fear was almost numbing. She looked back at Joe and found the tension in her muscles ease. He was like a balm for her nerves. He stood, his back to her now as he listened to the message a third time.

He had a really good back, she thought. A broad back. A strong, impossible-to-break back. Definitely the back of a man who wouldn't let anyone hurt her as long as he was around.

She'd been smart to hire him. Ridiculously dumb to fire him. The good news was he didn't fire easily.

Finally, after a fourth listen, Joe handed her the phone back.

"I've got a buddy at the FBI. I can have him record the message and then boost the sound quality to check for background noises. Even without a bunch of equipment I can tell you the voice at the end of the recording isn't live. It's taped."

"How can you tell?" The relief was palpable, and Vivian sat on the couch so he wouldn't notice how weak her legs were.

"The quality of it. It sounds like he's talking through a tunnel. Both messages were recorded and played into the phone. The re-

STEPHANIE DOYLE   89

cording of the interview was much higher
quality so you could hear it more clearly. Then
there's a slight clicking sound. As if someone's
hitting a series of buttons, and a few seconds
later you hear McGraw's voice."

Vivian winced at his name. She never liked
to think of him as an actual person with a
name. Instead he was a thing. An embodiment
of depravity, cruelty and evil. When he was
Harold McGraw, he was a man with a history.

He'd lost his wife and newborn during
childbirth. It was his third child. Perhaps losing her, left to raise two children on his own,
had changed him, broken him.

She thought about how sick he must have
been to do and say the things he did to her
and realized that sickness was a mental health
issue. She felt guilt over his death, and she
didn't want to feel guilty. Joe did what he had
to do to save her. There couldn't have been
any other ending.

Still he'd left behind two children, orphans
who would forever bear the scars of their father's infamy.

"Someone got a recording of his voice," she
concluded. It made sense. She'd been foolish
to think he was still alive. "How?"

Joe sat down next to her, his weight dipping the cushions so Vivian was practically touching him. "It wouldn't have been impossible. There was some footage of him, home movies. That sort of thing. Someone could have stolen it from a news station storage room. Or maybe whoever is doing this asked for footage on the premise of doing research. It's an old story. It's not like anyone cares about it anymore."

"I care," Vivian said.

"I didn't mean to downplay it," Joe said roughly. "I was there, too, remember. I'm just trying to sort this thing out."

"Which leads me back to my original question. Why were you outside my door? I thought I fired you."

Joe shrugged. "Yeah, well, I decided I'm tired of being sacked by Bennetts. Once in any lifetime is enough. I unfired myself."

"You unfired yourself," Vivian repeated, unable to stop the small smile from forming. It was a very Joe thing to do.

"You got a problem with that?"

Vivian shook her head. "No. I was coming to rehire you anyway. I was stupid to fire you when I clearly want the protection. It doesn't change the fact that you were an ass to me."

Another shrug. "If you're waiting for an apology…"

"I'm not," she said immediately. "I know better. The Joe Hunt I know…well, the Joe Hunt I knew, never apologized for anything. It was your personal motto."

"As mottos go, it's not a bad one. It basically means I try not to do anything I know I'm eventually going to regret."

"So you've never regretted anything?" Vivian wondered, almost astonished. There were so many things she regretted. Her perm in the eighth grade. Letting her father take her to the prom in high school. Telling Joe she loved him in the middle of a party and picking the bathroom of all places to do it. Running away from him that night. Nicholas.

Sometimes Vivian believed she regretted more things than she was proud of. At least she was on much firmer ground now. Mostly because she'd started taking real control over her life.

"I regret I let you go," he said after a moment, as if he couldn't stop the words.

Let her go. What did that mean? Did it

mean he should have fought to visit her in the hospital? Or maybe he regretted not trying to find her after she was released. Because that was exactly how she felt in the days and weeks after he'd left. As if she'd been holding on to him for years and suddenly he just let her go.

The horrible sensation of falling endlessly.

"I mean, you took off so quickly. If I had just grabbed your arm in time, I could have stopped you. Maybe I could have talked some sense into you."

Of course. He meant it in the literal sense. Vivian wanted to kick herself. When was she going to realize he hadn't felt for her what she'd felt for him? When was she going to stop looking at that relationship from so many different angles, trying to find out where she'd gotten lost in it?

Now, she hoped. Now that they were saying the things they both had needed to say back then.

Like how he regretted letting her go. It was a start. She patted him on the arm in a gesture of comfort.

"Well, don't beat yourself up. I was nimble."

"Nimble?"

"Yes, it was one of my skills. I didn't have a

lot of physical strength or gritty competitiveness for athletics like my father would have appreciated, but I was nimble. Light on my feet. Nimble and elusive. That was me."

He barked out a laugh.

"What?" she asked, wanting to know exactly what was so funny.

"You…elusive? You're the most obvious person I know. I'll give you nimble, sweetheart, but elusive just doesn't fit."

"I can be elusive. Maybe not CIA or Secret Service elusive," Vivian countered, suddenly offended that he was mocking one of her more fundamental talents. She was also trying not to focus on what he'd called her. *Sweetheart.* That was new. A line, even jokingly, he never would have crossed before.

"Get a grip, Viv."

"It's true. I have dodged groping staffers, drunken heads of state and clinging congressmen all without making a fuss. Without anyone getting upset. Without my father knowing. Take me to any state dinner in the land and I can find a potted plant to hide behind. One minute I'm hostess extraordinaire, the next I'm gone. That, my friend, is elusive."

"Okay, fine. You're elusive," he conceded,

although saying it made him chuckle again. "You hated those parties. I remember that. You were always a bundle of nerves before each one."

"Anyone who isn't trying to impress someone hates those dinners. Except for my father. He loved the pomp and circumstance. He loved to work the room."

"You didn't."

"No. I thought they were stuffy, overly formal and completely devoid of interesting conversation. Plus, any time I went to a political function I knew I was going to have to be 'on.' Being the first daughter was like playing a part, and it was a considerably bigger part for me since there was no first lady. I was always trying to be whatever it was they expected I should be. I wasn't that great of an actress, so instead I tried to blend into the background."

"You were too pretty to ever be part of the background. Especially when you were all dressed up."

She could feel her cheeks heat, blushing over a simple compliment like a teenager. Then again this was a compliment from Joe, and that was a rare thing. Like being called *sweetheart*.

"I remember you hated to wear your tux,"

she reminded him, nudging his shoulder. Maybe they could have this moment of shared memories without all the baggage between them. It was nice.

"Definitely one thing I don't miss about the job."

"Do you miss the rest of it? I know you didn't want to go back when Tom offered you the chance, but do you miss it?"

Joe was quiet, long enough she didn't think he would answer.

"I missed having a purpose. I had a set goal in mind, and each day was about meeting the goal. Every time you made it back to your dorm at night safely, I had accomplished something."

"You solve cases now. That's an accomplishment."

He shook his head. "It's not quite the same. There's not a lot of nobility in catching cheating spouses. Protecting the president's daughter. Putting your life on the line for her. For your country. That's noble."

"I'll ask it again. Surely not all of your cases are cheating lovers?"

"No, not all. There was this one case where a mother came in and wanted me to find her son. She was a single mom trying to raise a fourteen-year-old boy, and apparently things were getting out of hand at home. She tried to discipline him, and he took off. I found him a week later on the streets. He was half-starved and about to become a drug runner for the local street gang in order to pay for some food. I got him out of there just in time, scared the shit out of him and sent him back to his mom."

"You saved his life." Vivian smiled. "That was noble."

Joe looked at her then as if trying to read beyond her words. "I'm not a hero, Viv. Stop painting me as one or it will end up costing us both when I let you down."

"I don't think you get it. The only time you ever let me down was when you didn't say goodbye before you left."

He opened his mouth to reply, then closed it. Vivian supposed there really was nothing to say.

"So what happens next?" she asked, changing the topic.

"We try to get some sleep. Tomorrow we'll see my friend. He's stationed in DC. Then we have to start thinking about people you know who might want to terrorize you. And we have to consider this is some crackpot who saw you on the local news."

Vivian shook her head. "It doesn't feel like that. Like it's some random stranger. I don't know why, but it feels personal."

"Because someone is using your past against you. Trust me, we have to consider everything."

"I do," she said, and it was the truth. Regardless of their history, she knew she could trust Joe. "I won't be able to sleep, but you should take the recliner. It will be the most comfortable spot for you."

Vivian got up and took his cup with her to the kitchen.

"I don't like that," he said from across the room.

"Joe Hunt doesn't like something—there's a headline for the morning news," she said over her shoulder. "What don't you like?"

"You not sleeping."

"I have insomnia. It's not like I have much of a choice."

Joe got up and met her as she walked back from the kitchen. He looked down into her face, and she wondered how tired she looked. The bags were always there. A constant reminder of her sleeplessness, which she ruthlessly hid with concealer each morning.

Almost unconsciously, he lifted his fingers, as if maybe he could wipe them away like tears. Then his hand dropped, but something else flickered in his eyes, and he quickly looked away from her.

"I need you to be sharp. Alert. You can't be on just a couple of hours of sleep a night."

"I've made it this far," she protested.

"Up until now you weren't being stalked."

Stalked. The harsh reminder of why Joe was actually here. "I got a few hours of sleep earlier. I'll be fine."

"Don't you have pills or something you could take?"

"I do, but I only use them in an emergency, when I've gone days without rest. They really knock me out, and when I wake up I feel groggy the whole day. Trust me, if you want me alert, you want me drug free."

"Okay. But if I see that it starts to get bad, you'll take the pills."

She wouldn't argue. Not tonight. He looked tired despite the coffee, and she figured at least one of them should sleep. "I'll get you a pillow and some blankets."

When she returned with the bedding, she could see how quickly he'd made himself comfortable in the recliner. She handed him the pillow, and then in a weird instinct, she unfolded the blanket and spread it over him. Such a little thing. Vivian Bennett was taking care of big bad Joe Hunt. That was a switch.

"Good night, Joe."

She turned away from him, but he reached for her hand and clasped it firmly in his.

"Promise me you'll try to get some sleep."

She opened her mouth to tell him how pointless it was, but she could see his expression.

"You're not going to be able to make insomnia go away like a panic attack."

He couldn't fix her like he used to be able to do through sheer force of will. She probably should be annoyed he thought he could after all this time.

"Promise me," he said again.

But this was Joe. The Joe she used to know, who didn't seem much different from the man who was gently squeezing her hand and demanding the impossible.

"I promise," she whispered, telling herself she was saying it only to get him to let go of her hand. Touching him wasn't a good idea, even though it felt good. But even as she turned the lights out and took her Kindle back to her bedroom with her, she knew she would at least try to close her eyes and see if sleep might come.

Because she'd promised him, and apparently that still meant something to her.

CHAPTER SIX

"JOE HUNT. IT'S been a while."

Vivian and Joe had been waiting in the lobby of the J. Edgar Hoover Building when a tall, lanky man approached them. His hair was thinning up top and he wore thick glasses. Vivian's first thought was that he had the look of a tech guy. If he was a friend of Joe's, she knew he had to be competent. Joe didn't tolerate incompetence in others very well. Something he had in common with her father.

"Good to see you again, Bill. Sorry we lost touch," Joe said, shaking the other man's hand. "You remember Vivian Bennett."

"Of course. Ms. Bennett." Bill acknowledged her with a head nod.

"Please, call me Vivian."

"I have to say I'm a little intrigued by what this is about."

Vivian figured that was an understatement.

"Can we talk some place more quiet?" Joe

asked him. "We would like to keep this as private as possible."

"Sure. I won't be able to get you past security without authorization, but there is a coffee shop around the corner. Does that work?"

They made their way out of the building to the coffee shop and found an open booth in the back. Joe walked up to the counter to place their order while Bill sat across from her, clearly assessing her.

It was something a lot of people did when they first met her because it was hard to know what category she fell into. Helpless daughter of a powerful man, tragic victim of a kidnapping or spoiled sexpot and evil adulteress?

"Tell me, what do you do with the FBI?" she asked, not comfortable with the silence. "Are you a special agent?"

Vivian hoped the questions would make him focus and he would stop looking at her like she was some odd puzzle he needed to solve.

"Yes, and my focus is on technical analysis. I do a lot of sound work. Right now the FBI's primary focus is on homeland terrorism, so we do a lot of work breaking down recorded conversations. Although there is still the occasional kidnapping. You would be amazed at what our forensic psychologists can do with speech patterns. They can tell if the kidnapper's goal is money or if he's some kind of wacko in it for the kicks."

"Yes. I remember what a wacko kidnapper sounds like."

Bill's eyes nearly bulged out of his head. "Oh, hey, I'm sorry. I didn't mean to bring up…"

"It's all right," Vivian said. "I'm sorry. I shouldn't have made a joke of it."

Joe joined them at the table and passed Bill a paper cup. Vivian had asked for tea and used the opportunity to move past the awkward moment by focusing on steeping her tea bag.

"So why are you two here? Together?" Bill finally asked.

"Vivian's been getting some threatening letters. Last night someone left a recorded message on her home phone." Joe pulled out a USB drive from his coat pocket. He'd shown her this morning how to forward the message to her email account and from there download it onto the external drive. "I would like you to punch up the quality, take a listen to it and see if you can identify anything in the background. A voice, distinct noises. Anything that might help identify who made the recording."

"Why not go to the DC police?"

Bill was looking at Vivian when he asked the question.

"Vivian already notified them and they weren't much help," Joe answered for her. "You know how hard it is for cops to deal with stalkers. Until the perp makes a serious move, it's almost impossible to investigate. I would like to prevent any type of serious move from happening in the first place."

"Uh… I think you forget who her father is. He can get the Secret Service involved and then they can…"

"I don't want the Secret Service," Vivian said adamantly. "They have other, more important priorities. That's why I hired Joe."

"She trusts me," Joe said.

"Really?"

The astonishment was obvious in the agent's question.

Suddenly, the silence between the three of them then was thick. Vivian turned and saw Joe's jaw clench tight.

"Hey, I didn't mean it like that," Bill apologized lamely.

"Yeah. You did," Joe said tightly. Then he leaned over the table. "Let's cut to the chase, Bill. I'm sure you're very busy. I know your work takes precedence over a favor to an old friend. However, this is not a favor. You owe me, and you know it. Listen to the message. Tell me what you hear. If I don't have something from you in a few days, I'll give your supervisor a call. Let him know about the side projects you've been working on at home with government-issued equipment. You still doing that?"

"That's right," Bill muttered. "I forgot in addition to being an old friend you're also an unforgiving asshole."

"That's me." Joe stood and reached into his pocket. He pulled a business card out of his wallet and dropped it on the table. "Contact me at that number. If I don't answer, leave a message where I can reach you. Let's go, Vivian."

The polite thing would have been to say nice to meet you, and thank you for helping me, but the expression on Joe's face negated the need for any pleasantries.

"I do trust him," Vivian said, even as she slid out of the booth. "You don't understand what happened... It was my fault..."

"Vivian," Joe barked at her. "Let's go."

For a moment she considered giving him the finger just to aggravate him. Except she knew him too well. He wasn't mad, he was humiliated. A very hard pill for a man as proud as Joe to swallow.

"I trust him with my life," Vivian said over her shoulder even as Joe led her out of the coffee shop.

The day was sunny, but the temperature was frigid as winter gripped the city. Vivian tightened her coat around her and wished she'd thought of gloves. At least they didn't have the long walk to the Metro. Joe had decided they would take her car instead as he wasn't sure where the investigation might lead them. The thought of her heated seats was a small comfort.

Once they reached her SUV, Joe moved to the driver's side.

"You know I can drive," she told his back, the back she'd been looking at the entire walk from the coffee shop.

He shot her a look over his shoulder she

knew well and decided not to put up a fight and moved to the passenger side.

"So, tell me exactly how many *friends* do you have?" she asked as soon as she pulled the door shut.

"Just don't, Vivian." He started the car, and she reached for the heated-seat button. Then he pulled out into the late-morning DC traffic and they moved along the busy streets.

"Or maybe you don't have friends at all, just people who owe you."

"I said drop it."

"He didn't mean it."

"He did mean it. You know what's worse? He's right. Your hiring me to protect you is, to say the least, shocking. Most people would say it was stupid."

"Nobody else knows what happened," she insisted. "We do. We know it wasn't your fault. It was my fault. But you would never say that. You would never tell anyone what really happened."

A rough laugh escaped his throat. "And what the hell was I supposed to tell everyone, Vivian?"

He had a point. There was really no way to talk about what happened without embarrassing her. Still, there could have been some middle ground. A compromise of blame.

"You were so damn righteous. You played the martyr and you didn't have to. If you had just told them I ran away…"

"I let you go!" he shouted. Abruptly, he pulled the car out of traffic and into an open space along the street. He threw the gearshift into Park and turned to her, grabbing her shoulders so that she was forced to face him.

"I let you go," he said again as if she couldn't understand English.

"Because I kissed you. Because I was crying. You were trying to be sensitive. I understand it sounds ridiculous using that word in connection with you, but we both know that's the only reason you let me go."

"You idiot," he said with a laugh. "Is that what you think? You think I let you go because I was being sensitive to your feelings?"

He was laughing again, but there was no humor in it.

Then she remembered that moment when she felt him return her kiss. Those precious seconds she'd told herself over the years couldn't have been real.

"Tell me."

When he looked at her again, there was something in his eyes she'd never seen before. Then his hand was cupping her neck and he was pulling her toward him until their lips were a breath a part.

"You want to know why I let you go?" he asked, his voice low and ominous.

"I've been wanting to know that for ten years," she whispered back.

Suddenly all distance between them was gone and he was kissing her as she hadn't been kissed in ten long years. His kiss had a power that went beyond the punch of physical desire and touched her in a place no one else had access to inside her. No one except Joe.

Plus, he knew how to kiss. As he held her face, he controlled the angle of her head, the penetration of his tongue. Sometimes he teased her with soft lip-to-lip kisses until she was lulled into complacency and then he would strike, thrusting his tongue deep into her mouth, stealing her breath and robbing her of thought.

She couldn't think when Joe kissed her. She could barely breathe. She could only feel. The slick slide of flesh against flesh, the brush of his beard against her cheek, the heat of his mouth, the jagged tooth she knew he'd chipped during a high school hockey game.

It had been so long, and though there had been kisses between that first one with him and this one now, she now thought there shouldn't have been. She shouldn't have ever kissed anyone else because it always left her wanting. Always a distant runner-up to what she knew a kiss could be. This was how she was supposed to feel. With him giving her everything in him and her offering everything in return.

She felt him pulling away, and she reached out to grab his shoulders.

"No," she protested as his mouth left hers and speech was once again possible. "Don't do this again."

"Vivian," he whispered.

Just then a knock on the driver's side window caught their attention. Joe turned away from Vivian and hit a button. The window slid down and an officer poked his head inside. "You can't park here."

"Sorry, Officer. Do you need to see my license?"

"Just exit the spot."

"Thank you, sir."

JOE WAITED UNTIL the officer made it back to his car. He hadn't even noticed the cruiser. Hell of a bodyguard he made when he didn't see something as obvious as a police car with its lights flashing in his rearview mirror.

Of course, since his tongue had been halfway down Vivian's throat, it was only natural he was blind to everything else. He could still taste her, and it infuriated him. Hadn't he made this mistake already? Hadn't he paid for it for over ten years? What the hell was wrong with him?

"That wasn't an answer."

Joe barely looked over at her. He didn't want to see how swollen her lips were. He didn't want to think about what else he wanted to do to her mouth.

Damn her. She tasted so damn good.

"We're in a moving car so there's no running away from me," she said calmly. "Obviously I'm not going anywhere. And damn it, I want an answer."

Joe said nothing.

"I mean it, Joe. Say it! I deserve that much. I deserve the truth!"

He felt the punch to his arm, and this time

when he looked over he saw her face was red with anger.

"Why can't you just admit it?" She was screaming. Actually shouting at him in a way he'd never heard from her before.

"Fine," he snapped. "You want your damn answer. I let you go because I…because I wanted you. I wanted you so bad I was shaking with it. I wanted to lift you on that crappy bathroom sink, tear off your clothes and pound into you, until you forgot your name. Is that what you wanted to hear?"

He glanced at her. Her head was tilted back. Her eyes closed.

"I didn't imagine it," she whispered. "You did kiss me back. I wasn't crazy. I knew I felt something, but then you were gone…"

"You little idiot, look what it cost you! Do you even get what my stupid-ass crazy desire did to your life?"

"You couldn't have known he was going to be there that night…"

"I should have known!" Joe shouted. Mad at her for not understanding. Mad at her for making him relive every second of his failure. "You saw the pictures. He'd been stalk-

ing you for weeks. Weeks, and I never once
made him."

"He wore disguises."

Joe wanted to laugh again. She was defend-
ing him. She'd spent three days in hell because
of him, almost died because of him, and she
still defended him.

"Disguises I might have seen through if
I hadn't been so damn focused on you. You
were my job. My responsibility, and instead of
detecting the danger that was following you,
all I was doing was thinking about how not
to touch you. How not to want to touch you.
The second I felt it, the very moment I had the
thought in my head, I should have removed
myself from your detail. But I didn't. I didn't."

Joe slammed his hand on the steering wheel
in a fit of rage, and suddenly he was mad at
her all over again. Furious with her for making him remember how pathetic he'd been.
How selfish.

He'd been afraid of what admitting his feelings for her would mean for his career. How
his superiors would feel about him not being
able to maintain an emotional distance from
the people he was supposed to be protecting. It
was a reasonable concern. In his gut he knew

that was only part of the answer. He simply hadn't wanted to let her go.

Selfish. Asshole.

"You know, Joe, someday you're going to have to deal with the fact you're not impervious to being human. I know your father pounded it into your head that you needed to be perfect or nothing. This might hurt to hear, but frankly it makes being around you a little tough. Because no one is perfect. No one. You want to take all the blame for not knowing what was happening with McGraw. Not seeing him in the crowds. Fine. But there were always two agents assigned to me when I went out. Carl didn't spot him. You think that was because he was too focused on me, too?"

Carl had been married with a baby and another one on the way. And no, he'd obviously had no interest in Vivian like that. That was something Joe didn't even like to think about, because in some ways what Carl had done that night could have let Joe off the hook for being totally responsible.

Joe couldn't accept that. He had to own what happened to Vivian. It was his guilt to carry.

"Cindy was the point agent on your days

off and evenings. She never spotted him, either. Was that because she wanted me, too?"

He snorted then. "You're being ridiculous."

"You're being thick and stubborn. A bad thing happened to me on many agents' watch, Joe. Not just yours."

"I let you go," he said, feeling the anger run out of him.

"And you'll never forgive me for it, will you?"

He looked at her then and wondered if that was true.

She smiled sadly, nodding, as if he'd confirmed what she thought. "I'll take my consolation in knowing I wasn't crazy."

Yeah, it must have seemed that way to her at the time when he pushed her away. When he called her a child. She must have thought everything she'd ever felt had been one-sided. He realized how cruel he'd been.

"You weren't crazy."

She looked away from him. "What happens now?"

"I find out who is threatening you and I don't lose my focus. No matter what."

She turned back to him, and he could tell she understood what he meant. He wouldn't

be kissing her again. Not until this was behind them.

And then?

Joe didn't think he was ready to go there,
but he knew one thing. That had been one hell
of a kiss. Between two people who maybe had
too much history between them to overcome.

Or maybe not.

"Now it's my turn," he said. "You tell me
something." He hadn't even realized he wanted
the answer to the question he knew was none
of his business.

"What?"

"Nicholas. Why him?"

He watched her expression change. Shut
down. She didn't want to go there and he understood that, but the affair had never made
sense to him. He knew she didn't have it in
her to seduce a married man despite what had
been reported. Despite what Nicholas and his
wife had said. Except she'd never once con-
tradicted any accusation.

"You're asking the wrong question."

Joe waited.

She looked at her hands in her lap. "You
were gone and I knew you weren't coming
back. The question is, why not him?"

Joe let out a soft breath. He supposed he deserved that, but it still hurt. One more thing he could blame himself for.

"I don't want to talk about it," she said. "Can we just focus on something else? Something simple?"

"Sure."

She smiled again, and his insides felt warm to see that smile after all this time.

"Good. I'm starving. Find me something to eat."

CHAPTER SEVEN

"I DON'T KNOW what I want," Vivian said as she stared at the menu. They had picked a restaurant that was slightly more upscale from Dom's bar not too far from the Capitol. A hot spot for DC politicians and staffers. While it was a place to be seen, and to make connections, usually Vivian avoided it. But it also had really good food.

"There's a surprise," Joe muttered as he stared at his own menu.

It had been a common enough refrain when they used to eat out together. It always took her an agonizing amount of time to pick what she wanted to eat, mostly because she loved food and everything always appealed to her. One of the many things Joe used to grumble about whenever he escorted her to a restaurant. A food court could send her into a tizzy.

While she knew he would look at the menu for a minute or two and then order a burger, with Swiss cheese, medium rare and no tomato.

Joe hated tomatoes.

This was just one of the many things she knew about him.

As her body man, he hadn't been required to sit with her when in restaurants. He was supposed to secure whatever space she occupied and then keep to the background. Acting only if she was threatened in some capacity. Unobserved if possible, although how anyone failed to notice a man like Joe Hunt, Vivian would never understand. However, as they had gotten to know each other, it made sense to her for them to share their meals.

Vivian figured that was how it had started between them. Lunches and dinners that were better because she was eating with someone instead of alone. Talking about her day, listening to stories about his family. She'd loved every minute of those meals because she was with Joe.

Then it all ended with a kiss and a kidnapping, and the person who had been the biggest part of her life for two years, even if she was just an assignment to him, was gone.

Only he wasn't gone now. Now he was here

sitting across from her. Calmly, casually, as if that very big kiss in the car hadn't happened. As if he hadn't admitted to her he had shared her feelings ten years ago.

What did it mean? A new beginning? A flashback to the past?

Nothing?

Not nothing. Vivian knew that much. Heck, she was still reeling from it emotionally, so it wasn't nothing. She could still taste him in her mouth. She took a sip of her water.

"I can't decide between the fish tacos and the roast pork sandwich," she said, hoping she sounded calm and unaffected. After all, it was just a kiss.

Joe grunted and set his menu down. "I'm going to have a burger."

Vivian would have laughed if it hadn't made her sad to think about what might have been. What if he'd done what he said? Her panties were still damp from the words. What if he had lifted her onto that sink and pounded into her until she forgot her name?

What would have happened after that? She wouldn't have been kidnapped. He wouldn't have been blamed for it. But what would they have been? Vivian struggled to imagine them as a normal, happy couple. Just her and her bodyguard having an affair with nobody the wiser.

The waitress came over to take their orders. Vivian went with the fish tacos and listened as Joe ordered the burger exactly as she knew he would.

"What?" he asked her once the waitress had left.

She must have been staring at him. She couldn't help it. For ten years she'd told herself Nicholas had been at least partly right in his assessment of her. That her feelings for Joe must have been fantasy based. Hero worship. Because it couldn't have been any clearer that he didn't return her feelings. Made obvious when he'd pushed her away that night.

Sure, there had been that one moment. But it had happened so fast, she hadn't been able to convince herself it was real.

Vivian remembered having to repeat every awful word Joe had said to her that night during one of her early therapy sessions while Nicholas patted her hand, a look of pity in his eyes he didn't try to hide.

That look had made her, in a moment of desperation, tell Nicholas she'd thought Joe was lying. She thought he might have kissed her back. That he did have feelings for her. He was just angry that he had those feelings.

So Nicholas made her repeat the words.

Foolish. Idiot. Spoiled brat. Daddy's little princess.

Over and over until she had to face the truth. Which she eventually did. After all, if she'd meant anything to Joe, he would have tried to visit her in the hospital. He wouldn't have just left without a word.

Nicholas liked to remind her of that, as well.

Only now she knew she'd been right all along.

Vivian wanted to find Nicholas and punch him hard in the nose. The prick.

"I'm sorry, I'm still coming to grips with the fact that I wasn't crazy. All those times we ate together, that wasn't really part of your job, was it?"

Joe stiffened and sat back in his chair as if trying to create as much distance from her as he could.

Except it was too late, she thought. She knew the truth. He had wanted her.

No, present tense. He still did. She had

proof of that. She could still feel the bruise of him on her lips.

"Why didn't you have a pack of girls to run with?" he asked instead. "It was college."

He was deflecting the question, but Vivian could play along. "You know I had a hard time making friends. I never knew who was genuine or who wanted to use me because I was the president's daughter."

"Yeah. At first I felt bad for you. Poor little rich girl. All alone in the big White House. I figured it couldn't hurt to sit with you while you ate. You needed…someone to talk to. In hindsight, it was a mistake. It compromised my objectivity."

That hurt, but Vivian was starting to believe that pain was going to part of their journey. For both of them. Neither of them had forgotten the past, and neither had moved on from it. The wounds might have scabbed over, but they were still there. Maybe the only way to finally heal was to rip off the scabs and let the gashes they had inflicted on each other bleed cleanly.

"Is that how you think of me? When you do think of me, I mean. Or I should say *if*? *If* you think of me. As a big mistake? It would be understandable if you did."

Vivian braced herself.

For a moment Joe said nothing, then he met her eyes directly. "Vivian, I try very hard not to think of you every single day."

She laughed softly. "Yeah. Me, too."

"VIV…" JOE STARTED, but he really didn't know what he wanted to say. She was messing with his head in ways she hadn't done in ten damn years, and it made him nearly dizzy.

"Vivian!"

Joe looked over his shoulder at the sound of her name. The man approaching them in the cashmere coat screamed *politician*. He bent down to kiss her cheek, and he could see the faintest resistance before she offered him the side of her face.

Joe had an urge to growl.

"What a delightful surprise to see you here." He flashed shiny white teeth.

"You too, Jefferson. Let me introduce you to an old friend. Joe, this is Congressman Jefferson Caldwell. Jefferson, this is Joe."

"Hunt," Joe added because he wasn't going to hide. From anyone. "Joe Hunt."

He watched the congressman reach for name recognition. These people were experts in storing names and faces and recalling them at will. That was how they raised the big money.

"You'll get there," Joe told him as the man looked at him quizzically. Then his expression changed and he put on a somber expression, one Joe imagined Caldwell practiced in a mirror.

Yeah, he didn't like this guy even a little bit.

"Vivian, what are you doing here with this man?"

Vivian stiffened. "I told you, he's an old friend."

"You can't be serious." He bent then as if speaking only to her despite the fact Joe could hear him. "Were you coerced in any way?"

"You've got that backward, Jeff. She sought me out. Now we're about to have some lunch, if you don't mind."

The man's face puckered like he'd eaten something sour.

"Excuse my interruption, of course. I'm only here to pick up an order for myself and a few of my colleagues. Then it's back to work. At the Capitol."

Emphasis on the word *Capitol*. As if Vivian

had somehow forgotten the man was a congressman. Congressman Dick.

"But I'm glad to have had this chance to see you, Vivian. I don't know if you got my message last night, but I would love it if you accompanied me to the Horsham event on Friday…"

"Sorry, Jeff, that's not going to happen," Joe said before Vivian could respond.

She was glaring at him, but he didn't care. It was unlikely the situation with the letters would be resolved in a few days, and Joe wasn't letting her go anywhere without him.

"I'll be taking her." In case Congressman Dick didn't understand.

Jefferson looked at Vivian as if he couldn't believe she would support such an idea.

"Does your father know about this?" Jefferson asked her.

Ouch. Big mistake. Joe couldn't imagine that was going to go over well. Vivian was a thirty-year-old woman. He doubted she would appreciate the insinuation she needed her father's permission to date.

The Vivian he'd known had always wanted to be fiercely independent from her father. He wondered if that had changed after the kidnapping. He'd understand if it had. After what she'd been through, she deserved to be able to lean on someone. Since that wasn't him, it should have been her father. Except, he'd sent her to therapy instead.

When Joe had heard she'd moved to the other side of the country, he remembered thinking that that was his girl. Beaten, but not broken.

"I'm sure my father trusts my opinion on whose company I choose to keep," she said coolly.

Joe heard her loud and clear. That was political speak for *Go suck it*.

"Yes. Well, I'll be certain to seek you out. Hopefully we can find some time to talk."

The waitress arrived with their order, which was a perfect way to end the little powwow.

"Thanks for stopping by, Jeff," Joe said even as he gave his burger more attention. "Guess we'll see you Friday."

Jefferson smiled so hard Joe could see white. "Goodbye for now, Vivian."

The smooth man turned and went to the bar to pick up his order.

Joe tucked into his burger, not acknowledging the glare Vivian was continuing to give him. However, as soon the congressman left the restaurant, she started looking under the table for something.

"What did you lose?"

"I can't seem to find where you put your caveman's club. I was sure you weren't carrying it when we walked into the restaurant."

Joe smiled. "He needed to be shut down."

She rolled her eyes at him. "He's a decent man who didn't deserve your disrespect. You don't even know him."

"I know enough. He's a politician, and all politicians are untrustworthy scumbags."

Vivian opened her mouth to contradict him, but Joe held up a hand.

"With the exception of your father. He at least always spoke his mind and stood by what he said. President Bennett and I may have had our issues, but I never lost respect for him. Until he chose not to defend you against the press when they were making all those allegations of you being a seductress."

"That's not fair," Vivian said quietly. "What was he supposed to say? I had an affair with a married man. There was no paternal pride to be had there."

"You were broken," Joe said tightly. "And

your father knew it. He should have turned the focus back on the married bastard who abused his role as your therapist. Instead he shut his mouth. Someday he and I are going to have words about that, Vivian. You should be prepared."

Her eyes grew larger then. "You're making it sound like it's a given you're going to see my father again."

"He'll be at this Horsham event, right? I imagine I'll see him there."

Or earlier. Joe had no doubt that Congressman Dick would immediately report back to President Bennett about his daughter having lunch with him. Daddy was not going to be pleased. The congressman was at least right about that.

"Joe, I don't need you and my father fighting. Especially over something that happened so long ago. We should forget about the past and focus on what's happening right now."

"Speaking of which, when did you receive the first letter? Before or after you met Jeff?"

"He goes by Jefferson."

Joe smirked, telling her without words that he knew damn well the man went by Jefferson.

She thought for a minute. "About two weeks after I met him. Why?"

"He's interested in you and you are clearly not interested in him."

"You don't know that," she said, shifting in her chair and not meeting Joe's eyes.

"Vivian, an hour ago you let me stick my tongue down your throat. Ten minutes ago you barely let that guy kiss your cheek. You're not interested in him."

"Your point?" she huffed.

"If I was an up-and-coming congressman who wanted to leverage President Bennett's popularity, I might try to bag the daughter, too. If she wasn't interested, well then, maybe I might send some threatening letters to scare her a little. Then I'd swoop in and save the day. Offering protection and security. Get her to see me as a hero."

She rolled her eyes, but a smile teased her mouth. "That's a plot from a television show."

"Hey, some stuff on those political shows is based on real events."

Vivian shook her head. "You're crazy. Jefferson did not hatch some plan to scare me into dating him. He's not…original enough to try something like that."

Joe smiled and popped a fry into this mouth. "See, I told you. You're not interested him."

She pursed her lips. "I'm telling you it's not him."

"I'm keeping all my options open."

"Okay, well, I know I keep asking this, but what happens next?"

Joe watched as she took a bite of her taco. She closed her eyes and made a little humming sound, which meant it was delicious. That was the thing about Vivian, she embraced everything, relished everything and never thought about hiding her reactions. At least not when she was with him. He thought about what she said, how she handled herself at those state dinners and public events. He realized she was right. When she wanted to, she could fade into the background and be completely unobtrusive. Sharing nothing with anybody but a casual, if forced, smile.

But she was never like that with him. With him, she was always in the foreground. Because he'd put her there? Or because that was who she was when she was with him? Unafraid to be her true self.

It was why kissing her was like an explosion of sensation. In the past hour Joe had silently called himself every kind of fool for giving in to his desires. But even now, sitting across from her while she ate a damn taco, he wanted to swipe the table clear of plates and drag her across it to sit in his lap. He wanted her mouth again, he wanted her body. He wanted all of her. He told himself he could have none of it, not if protecting her and finding her stalker was going to be his first priority.

At least for now.

"What happens next?" she asked.

She probably wanted to know what steps he was going to take to find her stalker. Not about the kiss. Still, she'd let him into her mouth. Hell, she'd kissed him back…like she'd been waiting ten years for it.

"What does happen next?" he responded.

Her brow wrinkled. "That's what I asked you."

"I kissed you," he said and watched her blush delightfully.

"Yes," she said calmly even as she carefully wiped her fingers with her napkin like it was a very important task.

"You kissed me back."

"I did. See how easy it was to admit that?"

"What do *you* think we're doing, Vivian?"

She seemed hesitant when she answered. "You said you wanted to be focused. I took that to mean less kissing and more problem solving."

"Yeah, I know what I meant. I know what's smart. Logical. I know what rational decisions I should be making with my head and not my dick. But what do *you* want?"

The astonishment on her face gutted him. Because he instinctively knew it was something no one had ever asked her before. It made him understand she wasn't a twenty-year-old girl anymore. His to protect, his to direct, his to…control.

No, Vivian was an adult, a successful businesswoman, and he had no idea what she wanted for her life. To be safe, sure. To sleep, that was probably a given. But what did she want from him?

She smiled then, so bright it rocked him again. "Thank you. For asking."

"It wasn't my job back then to care about what you wanted," he pointed out. No, it had been his job only to protect her. Becoming her friend…that had just happened.

"I know. Besides, the reason people are always telling me what to do instead of asking me what I want is partly my fault. I let Daddy do it for too long. Then it became easy to let you do it, too."

"And your other relationships?"

Joe knew he was in trouble when he actually had to force the word *relationships* out of his mouth. He wasn't talking about Nicholas. That wasn't a relationship, in his opinion. Surely there were men after him, though. She was gorgeous and sweet. There had to be nice, normal men she'd met in Seattle.

Men who didn't let her get kidnapped and abused. Men who didn't abandon her.

"No, they were different. Or maybe I was different. I got better at asking for what I wanted. Making my own decisions. Having a business helped. I had no choice—I had to make every call."

Something dark washed over him. "But you didn't marry any of them."

Vivian shook her head slowly. "No, I didn't marry any of them. What about you? Couldn't find some nice, sweet, submissive woman to command?"

The word *submissive* made him think of

Vivian naked and tied to his bed. His to command, to pleasure. Yeah, that might be fun.

"No. Not even close to marriage," Joe admitted, shaking away the erotic thoughts. There had been women, some for a period of time. More for just a few hookups. He never looked at his failure to commit to someone too closely. However, in the context of Vivian's return, he might conclude that he'd been waiting for something. That the women in his life were merely placeholders until the main event.

"Joe Hunt, the lone wolf."

"I prefer living alone. Makes things less complicated." That at least was the truth. "You didn't answer my question. What do you want, Viv?"

"Oh. Well, that's easy. I have absolutely no clue."

Joe laughed because it was exactly like Vivian to be just that honest.

"Fair enough."

"Wait, I do want something. I would like you to come see my store. I need to check in with Angela anyway and, well… I want you to see it."

He thought about telling her he already had. He thought about what it would reveal about his feelings, and he realized that unlike Vivian, he wasn't ready to be so forthcoming.

"Sure," he offered. "Let's go see your store."

CHAPTER EIGHT

WHAT DID SHE WANT? As Vivian opened the door of her shop, happy to hear the bell above her head ringing, all she could think about was that question. She hadn't lied when she said she didn't have a clue.

She knew how she felt about seeing him again. She knew how it felt when he said something hurtful to her, when he kissed her.

She knew she wanted to kiss him again, even though he clearly was on the fence about whether that was a good idea.

Maybe it wasn't. Or maybe it was the answer to a ten-year-old question. Vivian considered what she knew now about what happened ten years ago. She was going to have to look at everything through a brand-new prism.

She remembered being so apprehensive about how he might receive her when she approached him that night. How angry he might be with her. Because she had to look at everything from what she thought was his viewpoint.

Based on his words, and because he hadn't seen her in the hospital, she imagined he was a man, recently fired, disgraced in front of his father, all because his assignment had fallen in love with him. None of those things had been his to control. Of course, she believed that all this time he must have resented her.

Although she could acknowledge that there was a part of her who always believed he was lying. Even if he was lying to himself.

Now she understood the truth.

Which meant she had to look at everything differently. When she had told him she was sorry in the bar yesterday, she thought she was asking forgiveness for kissing him and ruining his life. Now she knew her true crime had been forcing him to confront his feelings. Feelings he'd tried to suppress, that he didn't want. That would make him feel weak because he hadn't been able to control them.

Could he ever forgive her for that?

Vivian considered asking him, but she wasn't sure she was ready for that answer. It could wait. For now she wanted to show him what she had built for herself in the last ten years. She wanted him to see it and be proud of her. Which was probably ridiculous.

But so was seeking him out in the first place.

"Welcome to Vivian's Creations," she said as she stepped through the door and he followed. "Angela?"

"Hey." Her assistant came out from the back office with a friendly smile. A young girl with dark brown skin, hair and eyes, she was dressed in a bronze shirt that practically illuminated her. It was the first thing Vivian had noticed about her when Vivian interviewed her. Vivian could easily see how great personal style translated into good taste.

"Anything new come in?"

Angela smiled, looked over her shoulder and wiggled her eyebrows. "That."

Vivian turned to see Joe looking at a replica Louis Quinze chair that would most likely crumble underneath him if he chose to sit in it. Which thankfully he seemed to understand because he hadn't even touched it.

"Angela, this is an old friend, Joe."

Angela had been only thirteen when the kidnapping happened and had confessed she hadn't known much about it. Vivian had filled her in on the general details to explain why the letters sent to the shop were threatening, but she hadn't mentioned who Joe was.

"Joe, this is Angela. Hiring her was the smartest thing I've done all year."

"Hi, Joe," Angela said warmly as she offered her hand, and Vivian could see Joe was a bit bemused at her cordial reaction. It was the first time someone had seen them together without judgment.

No surprise. Just acceptance.

"Nice to meet you," he said, looking around the store that was filled with all kinds of pillows, chairs, end tables and wall hangings. "There's a lot of nice stuff here."

Angela smiled "Yep. We specialize in good *stuff.* Are you here looking for something in particular? Maybe a consultation?"

"No, Viv and I are just…catching up. She wanted to show me her store."

"He's also a private investigator," Vivian told Angela. "He's looking into the letters."

"Oh, awesome. I didn't want to tell you… I mean I saw how upset you were with the other ones…but if he can actually do something to stop this…"

A knot of dread formed in Vivian's gut. "Another letter?"

Angela shook her head. "A package."

"Where?" Joe said.

"I put it in the safe," Angela said, pointing to the back room she had come from. "I knew I couldn't throw it out in case you wanted to give it to the cops. It's nothing really. So stupid."

"When did it come in?"

"It was by the front door when I arrived this morning. Just a brown wrapped package, addressed to you. I didn't think anything of it really until I noticed it didn't have any postage on it or a return address."

Joe was already walking toward the back of the shop with Vivian close behind. She pushed him out of the way and spun the dial on the small safe they used to secure any daily cash transactions.

Angela was right. It was an innocuous cardboard box. Joe then moved Vivian out of the way and opened the top of it. Inside was some dirt. On the lid of the box more magazine letters.

I have dug myself out of the grave for you, Sugarplum.

Vivian could feel the air backing up in her lungs as she read it, but she didn't want to have a panic attack. Not in front of her employee. Angela didn't need to know she was working for a coward. She willed herself to take deep breaths through her nose until the panic subsided.

When it was over, she looked down to see she was holding Joe's hand. Or he was holding hers. She couldn't tell. All she knew was that it helped.

"Okay?" he asked.

She nodded and continued to focus on her breathing. Angela was right. It was a stupid stunt. Some dirt and words that meant nothing. Vivian found herself getting angry. Someone wanted her to be afraid, and that someone was a mean, slimy jerk.

Joe lifted the box and studied it, searching for anything that might give away its origins.

"Do you have Carl's number?"

Vivian had to think for a second. "Yes. From when he called to tell me he'd been to see you."

"Call him now. Tell him to come down to the shop."

"I don't really want the Secret Service involved," Vivian said tightly. "That was Daddy's idea. If this blows up or word gets out, it would be bad for my business."

"Word," Angela said from behind them. "No one wants to buy decorative pillows from someone if they think some crazy dude is going to be lingering around the corner."

Joe overruled them both. "Sorry, but I need access to their equipment. They can analyze the dirt, look for any traces of chemicals or something that might indicate where it's from."

Vivian huffed. "Joe, that dirt could from anywhere."

He shrugged. "I need everything I can get. This, whatever this is, isn't stopping. Letters, phone calls, now packages. He's upping the game, and I'm not taking any chances. Call Carl."

Vivian pulled her phone out of her purse and did as she was told. She thought about reminding him that he should be asking her what she wanted, not telling her what to do, but she also knew when it came to her safety he would be inflexible.

Joe didn't care about her losing potential customers. He wanted to find whoever was doing this. It is what she hired him for after all.

FORTY MINUTES LATER they heard the bell ring over the door. Angela walked out to greet the newcomer in case it was a customer. When she came back to the office she was followed by Carl, whose eyes immediately went to Joe.

"Hunt? What the hell are you doing here?"

"I hired him," Vivian explained. "As an investigator who has obvious connections to my past. I thought he could help."

"And you agreed to this?" Carl asked Joe, clearly incredulous. "I'm sorry, man, not for nothing, but she sort of destroyed your career. I would have thought… I suppose I wouldn't have thought you two would have anything to do with each other."

"Why do I feel like I'm missing something?" Angela interjected.

Vivian sighed. So much for having an unbiased friend getting to know Joe. "Joe was the point agent on my Secret Service detail the night I was kidnapped."

Angela's eyes got wide. "Oh, snap. Straight up, this is like something out of one of those fiction-but-based-on-true-events shows. I've always said real life can be way better than what's on TV."

Joe looked at Angela. "I knew I liked you."

The bell to the store rang again, and Vivian gave Angela a pleading look.

"Okay, I'm on it. But this story is not over. I want to hear all the details."

"Can we focus on why I had Vivian call you?" Joe asked. He moved aside and let Carl see the package on the desk. Carl walked over to it, opened the lid and read the note.

"Freaking creep," he muttered.

"Vivian!" Angela popped her head back into the office. "Sorry, but this could be a whale. New brownstone in Georgetown looking for a head-to-toe."

Vivian looked at Joe, and he nodded. "Go handle your business. We got this."

Joe thought she looked relieved to have an excuse to get away from the box. As if by being near it was enough to contaminate her. Joe wanted to physically hurt the person who made her feel that way.

"I'm going to need the analysis on the dirt."

Carl looked at him. "That's a long shot and you know it."

"When you've got nothing, you have to take everything you can. Like, say, interviewing me as a suspect."

"Person of interest. And that was Thompson's idea."

"Where is the puppy?"

"Working another case. Despite the former president's concerns, we've got other pressing matters that take priority over some letters."

"Take the box, Carl. Find out what you can." Joe didn't have to remind him how much Carl owed him for taking the heat over the kidnapping. "You know how to get in touch with me."

"Yeah, I know. I'll see what I can do, but so far nothing has come back on the letters. No prints, no special watermarks, standard stock paper. Nothing that points in any particular direction."

Except Joe thought that it did provide a clue: whoever it was knew how to be careful.

"Someone is doing this," Joe said tightly. "Someone who knows how to scare her the most. Vivian thinks it might be personal."

Carl shook his head. "I still can't believe you are here in this store. Is this about that little thing you two had ten years ago? Tell me your being here isn't so you can finally nail her after all this time."

Joe's first reaction was violence, but he

checked himself. Not that he was concerned about losing a fight. He'd always been quicker than Carl. However, he was certain Vivian wouldn't appreciate the two men fighting in her back office while she was dealing with a client. Think of how many fancy knickknacks they might break.

Instead, he used his soft, threatening voice. "You're going to want to watch what you say, Mather."

The man seemed agitated, as if he truly couldn't believe Joe would have considered forgiving Vivian for what happened that night.

"She was a twenty-year-old girl with a damn crush who flaked on us and cost us both our careers. Maybe I didn't lose my job, but I lost any hope I had of making it onto a presidential detail, and Bennett's opinion of me was made very clear to everyone even after he was out of office."

Joe didn't want to go there, but if Carl was calling out Vivian for the events of that night, then he needed a trip down memory lane.

"You should have lost your job, and we both know it. It wasn't her fault. It was mine for letting her go. But maybe…just maybe…if you hadn't been getting a blow job from some drunken coed in the backyard, you might have been out front when she came running out of the house."

Carl's mouth twisted into a sneer. "Yeah, I was waiting for that. You've always had that in your back pocket. Sure, you took the blame, kept my name out of it. Let me think you were doing me a favor. But it's always been there. Hasn't it? Waiting for just the right opportunity to crush me with it."

Joe thought of what he'd told Bill the other day. It wasn't that he'd planned to use the information he had against anyone. He'd considered Carl a friend at one point. He'd accepted 100 percent of the blame as well as the president's ire. In Joe's opinion, Carl's actions, while unprofessional, hadn't rivaled Joe's mistake in having feelings for Vivian in the first place.

Carl had a pregnant wife and a kid at home. One word from Joe would have destroyed the man's entire life, not just his career. At the time he didn't see the point. Now Vivian's safety was at stake, and there wasn't anything Joe wouldn't do to guarantee it.

"You're wrong, Carl. I haven't been holding it like some ace in my sleeve. Truthfully, I hadn't given it a single thought in the last ten years. But she's in trouble, and I need someone who has access to what I don't. Now, are you going to investigate this case, or do I need to start talking about what really happened that night to people who would still be interested in hearing it? I bet the puppy would be so disappointed in you."

"You're a real asshole."

"I get that a lot."

"I'll do everything in my power to find out who's sending these letters. That enough for you?"

"I guess it has to be."

Carl picked up the box, gave Joe the finger with this free hand and left. Joe wondered if he'd done the right thing by bringing up the past. It had been such a surreal moment when he'd gone looking for her. Shouting at drunken partygoers asking if they had seen her. The one girl describing how some guy just took her.

Just took her.

Joe didn't think he would ever forget the

bloodcurdling fear he felt in that moment. Then racing around to the back of the house to look for Carl, who had a girl on her knees in front of him. It hadn't really registered then. He'd been too frantic over tracking down Vivian. He'd shouted some orders at the agent, told him Flamingo had been taken, then started interviewing everyone who might have seen anything.

It hadn't been until later, until the FBI had been brought in and her father had been notified, that Carl had pulled him aside and asked Joe what his intentions were.

"To get her back."

It was how he'd answered him because it had been the only thing on his mind at the time. To get her back. His concern over Carl and what he'd been doing were insignificant. The only thing that had mattered was Vivian.

When Carl pressed him on the subject, it was easy to wave him off. To promise the older agent he wouldn't say a word and trust that it was a one-time incident that shouldn't end a man's career and marriage. None of that had mattered when Vivian was missing. Then they'd found her, and Joe had been fired. There didn't seem any point in divulging Carl's transgression.

Joe had his own secrets. He'd never told anyone about the kiss. His official statement when he'd filed the report was that they had argued over her drinking. He told her she was acting like a child, which upset her and caused her to leave his line of sight. He didn't immediately try to reengage contact because he wanted to give her a chance to cool down.

A breach of protocol. A failure to secure his charge. The result was her kidnapping.

Vivian came back into the office. "So what did you do to piss off Carl?"

He looked at her then and had a crazy urge to hold her. To put his arms around her and never let her go. Ever. He wondered if she might call the police on him if he suggested handcuffs that would permanently connect her to him.

"I told him to do his job better."

Vivian smirked. "Yep. That would do it. You know, in one day I've seen you tick off three different men. That might be a record."

"Nah. Four is typical. Three means I'm on my good behavior."

"Well, the day is not over yet."

"For you it is," Joe decided. "Did you finish up with your whale?"

"Angela is signing the paperwork with him now. Why?"

"We need to head back to your place and pack a bag."

"Why?"

"I don't want you staying there. Whoever this is obviously knows your place of business, but the message on the home phone means he most likely has your home address, too. Safest bet is to be in a safe location."

"And that is where? Some hotel?"

A hotel would be the logical choice, only Joe wasn't feeling very logical. Not when it came to Vivian.

"No. You'll stay with me."

He could see her consider it. He didn't think he liked the hesitant expression on her face. Like she was questioning whether that was a good idea.

"Is that going to be a problem?"

Finally she shook her head. "No. Not a problem."

"Good," he said a little stiffly. "Let's go."

Before he changed his mind and did something crazy like ask her for her opinion on handcuffs.

CHAPTER NINE

"MY PLACE MAY not be in the greatest shape," Joe warned as he unlocked his door.

"Your place? A mess. Really?"

That was a surprise to Vivian. Joe had been a neat freak. It was something they shared. Although their reasons for their compulsive neatness were quite different.

She liked a tidy room in order to show off her decorating style to its best advantage. He was simply a West Point graduate who had developed good habits in the military.

The apartment itself was a converted third floor of a brownstone, and as she stepped inside she instinctively started looking at the open space with a critical, professional eye.

"You know, if you pulled out this carpeting, I bet you would find hardwood floors underneath," she said absently as she walked through the space. "Even if it's a darker-stained wood, it would be better than this beige wall-to-wall carpet you have. It would make the space seem larger."

Joe shook his head. "It's a one-bedroom apartment. The only way to increase the size of this space is to knock out a wall."

"Not true. A white sofa with some colored throw pillows would be better than that." She pointed at the black leather sofa he currently had pushed up against a wall. "A ceiling fan. Perhaps a different color besides the stark white on the walls, maybe something in a very pale shade of blue or gray."

"Wait, let me get my notebook out. I'm going to need to write this down."

She gave him a look and he smiled.

He held his hand out for her coat and hung it, along with his, on an old-fashioned coatrack that suggested he wasn't unaware of style. It was actually a rather fun piece of furniture.

"Spaghetti and meatballs okay with you?" he asked as he moved toward the small galley kitchen. "Let me rephrase. There is no option. It's all I know how to cook."

Vivian followed Joe and saw a coffee mug in the sink. Something he must have left yesterday morning. It was the only thing that looked out of place in the apartment. She lifted it to show him. "You heathen."

He smirked and took the cup from her, placing it back in the sink.

"Do you mind if I look around while you get dinner ready?"

"Can I stop you?"

Vivian considered that for a moment. "No. It's not personal, you understand. It's just that as an interior decorator I feel it's my duty to scope out all homes I visit. Occupational hazard."

He shrugged. "Do your worst."

Vivian meandered around the living room. There were no knickknacks. No miscellaneous pieces. There was a lamp, an overhead light. A brown chair, a TV tray, the black couch and a really big flat-screen TV.

"Men," she muttered under her breath. There was a bookshelf on the far wall that was crammed with books of various sizes and colors. It was the only element in the room that lent any character to the space other than the coatrack.

Until she checked the titles. Other than a few paperbacks scattered throughout the shelves, everything else was related to the

FBI, CIA, Secret Service, murder, kidnapping, terrorism and death. Light reading for
Joe Hunt.

"Okay, sauce is warming and I put the pasta
in," Joe announced. "It should be a few minutes. You want a beer?"

"Sure," Vivian answered as she wandered
down the hallway to his bedroom. Taking a
peek inside, she found a large queen-size bed
with a dark green flannel comforter, a night
table and a dresser.

The bed was made. The dresser was clear of
any clutter, and an alarm clock was the only
thing on the night table.

Vivian made her way back to the kitchen
and took her beer from the counter where Joe
had left it for her.

"I could also recommend a few color-
coordinated throw pillows for the bed," she
said.

"Why?"

"To make it look prettier."

"What's the point? I'm the only one who
sees it, and I don't give a damn what it looks
like. If I have a date, we usually go back to
her place."

"Right," she said, trying not to be jealous of the women in his life and failing.

"Do you need a glass?"

She stared down at the bottle. "I can get one."

He laughed and pulled a glass down from the cabinet and handed it to her. "It's not a challenge, Viv. It's a beer."

"I suppose I'm more of a wine person."

"Ya think? 'I'll have a Chardonnay,'" he said in a raised falsetto with a bad British accent.

"That sounds nothing like me."

"It was close."

Vivian sniffed at him, then sipped at her beer, which was actually quite tasty. What he lacked in decor he made up for in beer and food. The meatballs he was pulling out of the fridge were premade, but Vivian knew the Italian deli where they were from. She watched as he dropped them into the pot of sauce on the stove.

"Joe Hunt cooking for me. Put that down in a category of things I never thought would happen again."

"Again?"

"You don't remember the sandwiches? You

used to make extra and feed me during my class breaks. Mostly because I think you secretly hated the cafeteria."

"I did hate the cafeteria. Too many people. Too many ways in and out. And it was always so loud."

"Plus, you were cheap," she accused him.

"I saved a lot of money on my daily food allowance…this is true. It was win-win for me. Besides, I thought you liked eating in the quad." It had been an outside section off the cafeteria with tables and benches. Never as many people around.

"I liked eating with you, Joe. It didn't matter where we were."

Carefully, he set down his beer, and Vivian thought this was definitely a strange new world they were both occupying. One where they were honest with each other about the past. She decided she liked it and she wasn't backing down from it.

"I missed you. After you were gone," she confessed. "Am I allowed to say that?"

"I missed you, too, Viv." His voice was rough and he wouldn't look at her, but she knew he would have missed her. She had been confident in their friendship at least.

It's why it had hurt so much when he left without a word. Not even a goodbye. She got it now, he'd been fired. But to just leave her without any word, not even a phone call— she couldn't pretend it hadn't hurt. Didn't hurt still.

She didn't want to talk about that, though. "So you're going to feed me and ply me with drink. What else are you going to do to keep me entertained?"

It had been a throwaway comment. Something to break the tension that had formed between them, except when she looked at him he wasn't smiling. In fact, he was nearly smoldering. It was right there on his face. He knew exactly what he wanted to do to her.

"I didn't mean... I just meant if you had any DVDs or something for later." Vivian tugged on her earring and glanced away from him. But she could still feel his eyes on her. Watching her. Assessing her reaction. She could feel him wanting her, which only made her want him back.

"Viv..."

"How are we going to do this?" she suddenly asked. "How are we going to spend day and night together and do this? Or should I say not do this?"

"We did it before," he pointed out. "For two years."

True. He'd wanted her back then, but he hadn't touched her. Not once.

"I cracked. Remember?"

"You're a more experienced woman now. You know that with sex comes consequences."

"True. I learned that the hard way."

Joe rubbed a hand over his face like he was trying to scrub a memory from his brain.

"Viv, we have no business even thinking about going down that road. One, I wasn't bullshitting when I said I need to remain focused on your safety. That has to be my priority. Two, it's obvious neither one of us has gotten over the past for a lot of different reasons. I'm not going to pretend this isn't confusing for me, too. But the odds of making it through everything that happened between us… I'm not going to lie. It doesn't look good for a possible future together."

"Not a one-night-stand kind of guy, huh?" She didn't know why she was asking. She wasn't a one-night-stand kind of woman.

"Not a one-night-stand kind of guy with

you. If I take you, if I have you…it's not going to be for one night. I think we both know that."

Vivian swallowed her beer and tried not to think about what that might be like. Night after night in Joe's arms. In his bed. But he was right. Starting down that kind of a path without having the past resolved would be disastrous. She'd promised herself she would avoid disaster after the debacle with Nicholas.

It didn't make her want him any less. After ten years apart and a couple of days together now, nothing had changed. Kissing him reminded her what actual passion felt like. Passion that was undeniable.

"Okay, then maybe we should watch a really, really sad movie. Always a turnoff for me."

"I was thinking of something with a lot of guns and shooting. If I remember correctly, you love those movies." Then he looked at her with what she hoped was an innocent expression. "Wait. Did you only say you like those movies because I liked them?"

What woman in the universe hasn't lied about liking something to impress the man she was interested in? The key was never admitting it.

"No, of course not, I love those movies. Pasta is probably done, don't you think?"

He was giving her a look. The Joe-Hunt-I'm-not-buying-your-shit look. "You're a crappy liar, Viv."

"Yes, but I'm a hungry crappy liar. Fish tacos were hours and hours ago."

As distractions went, it worked well enough. She set about his kitchen trying to find plates and silverware while he combined the sauce, meatballs and pasta into one large bowl.

It wasn't fancy but it was tasty, and for now they were both focusing on eating to keep the sexual tension at bay.

"Tell me something about your life now," she said over a forkful of pasta.

"What do you want to know?"

"Well, you said I don't know who you are anymore, which means you must have changed. I know you have your own business, a nice apartment—if not very fashionably furnished—that you date but there is no one serious. I know you have good taste in Italian delis and you can boil water and warm up sauce."

He grunted. "I don't know that there's much more to me than that."

"Were you sorry you never reconciled with your father?"

"Oh. You meant you wanted to know the serious stuff."

"I want to know *you*. That means figuring out what happened to you in the last ten years."

"Why? Why can't I just be your hired bodyguard who happens to feed you?"

That would be easier. Stony silence between two people who used to know each other. In the years since he'd left, she'd done a lot of growing up. She was more confident, had become more comfortable at developing friendships. She wasn't in the same position she'd been in back then when he'd been her world.

Her only friend.

So, no, she didn't need to get to know this 2.0 version of Joe Hunt. She wanted to, though. "Humor me."

Joe shrugged. "I guess I feel resigned to it. He's gone and I can't change it."

"Did you go to the funeral?"

He nodded. "I wouldn't have done that to my mother. She told me deep down he never stopped loving me. I thought that was crap. If he'd loved me he wouldn't have kicked me out of his life. Then I realized that's just who he was. It was black or white. Hero or villain. And in some ways, after leaving the service, after knowing I had nothing to prove to him anymore…it was like I was…"

"Free," Vivian said, supplying the word she knew he was searching for. That was exactly how she had felt in Seattle. Sad in many ways, but able to breathe for the first time, free of expectation.

"Yeah. I stopped making every decision based on whether or not he would approve. If I was a hippie, I guess you could have said I found myself."

"Joe Hunt, hippie? I'm not buying it."

He chuckled. "No, the hippie thing wasn't really my gig. I guess that's something you still know about me. I like structure. I like control. That's why I like owning my own business."

"And what does the future look like for Joe Hunt?" She had meant related to his business, but as he put his fork down and gave her that look again, she realized he thought she was asking something else.

"Just like you said. I don't have a damn clue.

What about you? Surely your father wants grandchildren."

Vivian rolled her eyes. "Oh, yes. Hence Jefferson. He doesn't think I really recovered after…well, all of it. He keeps playing matchmaker in the hopes I'll stumble into love before I realized what's happened, and if that happened to be with a politician who has a bright future, so much the better."

"That sounds like President Bennett. Exerting his influence in subtle yet not so subtle ways."

"He means well."

"Is he right? Are you still not recovered… from all of it?"

Vivian shrugged.

"You don't sleep." He said it like an accusation.

"Lots of people suffer from insomnia."

"Lots of people weren't kidnapped and tortured for days," he said grimly. Then as if he needed to move, he looked at her plate. "You done?"

She nodded and he stood to clear both plates. While he was cleaning up in the kitchen, she made her way to the refrigerator for another beer. The first had taken the edge off her tension. The second might actually make her relaxed enough to get some sleep tonight. One thing was for sure, she felt particularly safe. No small feat after receiving that package.

Joe was here, though, and that meant nothing bad was going to happen to her tonight.

It did raise a question. "What are the sleeping accommodations? You mentioned this is a one-bedroom."

"I'll sleep on the couch and you'll take my room."

Sleep in Joe's bed, on his sheets, under his blankets. Yeah, that wasn't going to happen. "Uh, it's better if I take the couch. Even if I do sleep, it's usually in spurts. I would rather have the whole apartment to wander around than to be stuck in a room."

"Okay."

Vivian plopped down on the couch and studied the remote control. She flipped on the television and started searching through the guide. "Oh, it's my favorite Christmas movie."

"I'm not watching a Christmas movie. They're all sappy and sentimental," he said.

Say what he wanted about not knowing who

he was anymore, Vivian wasn't buying it. Joe really hadn't changed all that much.

Then it occurred to her how vulnerable she was. Because she'd loved who Joe Hunt had been back then.

"Fine, guns and explosions it is," Vivian muttered, resigned to her fate. She handed him the remote and watched him look at the space next to her on the couch, then back at the only other chair in the room. Which didn't face the television. Probably a place to sit when he wanted to read.

Still, she knew he was considering moving it.

"Really? I promise not to bite."

"Maybe you're not the one I'm worried about," he said, not even trying to hide his thoughts.

"What's the matter, Joe? You scared?"

"Of you? Yes. Very much."

Vivian couldn't help but smile. "That's the sweetest thing you've ever said to me."

"Move over," he finally grumbled. She scooted to her side of the couch and felt the dip as he sat down. He hit a few buttons on the remote, and the next thing she knew she was watching some hit man who raced cars on the side and who had to save a girl.

She never found out if he managed to pull it off because somewhere in the middle of all the shooting and car racing, she fell asleep.

JOE STARED DOWN at her and shifted the blanket over her. He thought about waking her up so she could change into her pajamas but decided insomniacs were to be treated like fussy babies. If they managed to fall asleep you left them alone.

He wasn't necessarily tired, but it probably made sense to go to his bedroom. Let her get as much sleep as she could on her own. Yet he did none of that. Instead he sat back down on the couch close to her and settled her head on his thigh. She didn't so much as stir. Just continued her soft in-and-out breathing.

He picked up a lock of hair, so pale and fine. *That only God, my dear, could love you for yourself alone and not your yellow hair.*

Yeats knew what he was talking about.

He liked the weight of her on his body. Liked the idea she'd been comfortable enough with him to fall asleep.

Whom the hell was he kidding? He liked that she was here at all. With him.

He hadn't been lying when he said he had no clue what was coming next for them. Sex really would compromise him and would make an already complicated situation that much more so.

But he had been deluding himself if he thought for one second he could keep her at arm's length indefinitely. She had been right. The two of them together, day and night. A platonic relationship, while smarter, simply wasn't sustainable.

That kiss! He leaned his head back and tried simultaneously to block it from his mind and relive every second of it.

He didn't consider himself much of a romantic. Like any man, he liked sex and had enjoyed a number of women over the past ten years. Yet nothing had come close to feeling like what he'd felt with her in the car today.

No orgasm had ever been as intense as the taste of her, the feel of her in his arms again after so long.

In the last ten years, he'd rarely let himself remember the kiss they'd shared the night of the party. There was too much pain and awfulness associated with everything that happened afterward. Because when he remembered it, as intense as it had been, he also had to remember what she had looked like when he found her. Naked, rope burns across her body, beaten and bloody.

Now he had a new memory. A new kiss. A new moment with her fast asleep on his thigh. Sleeping, something she said she didn't do.

She did stir then, only to settle in more comfortably, with her hand now resting just above his knee.

Joe suddenly understood two truths.

One, he wasn't getting up and going to bed. He was going to stay on this couch all damn night and watch her sleep just because he could. Just like he'd done ten years ago, when he knew the smart move would have been to take himself off her detail but he didn't. He'd been stubborn and selfish.

Because he wanted to be with her. Because she was Vivian.

Apparently that hadn't changed in ten years either.

Two, he knew he had lost. Because when she woke up tomorrow, he planned to make a complicated situation a whole lot more complicated.

CHAPTER TEN

VIVIAN WAS WARM, deliciously warm. The kind of warm that could happen only in winter when you knew it was blistering cold outside, but you were tucked away inside safe and sound.

Beyond the coziness was a feeling of contentment. The kind she typically felt after getting more than three hours of sleep. She was pressed against something hard and unyielding, and it wasn't until she opened her eyes that she realized it was Joe. He must have dozed off, too, and somehow they had positioned themselves side by side on the couch with her practically sprawled over him.

Except there was a blanket thrown over them. So he had considered that before he'd fallen asleep.

Uh.

He was still soundly sleeping, his mouth open and soft sounds coming from his nose.

It was the most vulnerable she had ever seen him, and she relished it. She popped her chin on the hand that was resting on his chest and simply watched him.

A warning sign if there ever was one. But he was asleep and there was no one else here to judge her. For minutes she stayed that way until the discomfort of a full bladder annoyed her enough to move.

Carefully, without disturbing him, she lifted herself up. The blanket fell away, and she realized he was wearing a pair of flannel pajama bottoms and a T-shirt.

He'd changed before falling asleep on the couch.

Which meant she had already been asleep when he'd gotten up, gotten undressed and joined her on the couch before throwing a blanket on top of them.

Vivian made her way to the bathroom and addressed her first issue. On her way past the kitchen, she saw on the microwave clock it was a little after four in the morning. Definitely one of the longest nights of sleep she'd had in years. Since she was still in her jeans and Joe had looked so comfortable, she decided to change into her pajamas. Her bag was just in his bedroom, so she shucked her clothes and pulled on her bottoms and a long-sleeve T-shirt. She found her hairbrush and toothbrush.

Then she made her way back to the bathroom. She was brushing her teeth when she heard a noise behind her. She'd left the bathroom door open, and she could see Joe's reflection in the mirror.

He walked in behind her and took the toothbrush out of her hand, and in a moment of shocking intimacy he started brushing his own teeth with it. Vivian watched helplessly, until she realized she had a mouth filled with toothpaste. She rinsed her mouth and he followed, and then he put the brush in the dish alongside his.

It was surreal.

And it wasn't.

He wrapped an arm around her, and she was helpless to watch them both in the mirror as his hand slid slowly down until he tucked under her shirt and brought it up to cup her breast.

She watched as her nipples got hard under his fingertips and couldn't help the noise she made as she leaned her head back against his chest and let the pleasure roll through her body.

"When did you decide?" she asked as his hand slid from one breast to the other.

"Last night."

"And I'm just supposed to go along with this?"

He pinched her nipple and she gasped again, feeling the tug all the way through her body.

"Isn't this what you wanted?"

"I've wanted this since I met you, but you've always said no."

"I'm done saying no. Look at yourself," he whispered into her ear.

She opened her eyes and watched as he bent down and bit her exposed neck with enough pressure to make her shudder. Then she watched as his other hand came around her hips and dipped into the loose cotton pants.

He didn't tease, he didn't hesitate. His fingers were there feeling how wet she already was, pushing against her, finding her clit until she jumped. Then he was sliding fingers inside her even as he twisted and teased her nipples until finally she couldn't bear it.

"Joe, stop... I'm going to..."

"Come." It was a command.

She was helpless against his fingers, his mouth. She pushed her body back against him, her butt grinding on his erection, and she was there so fast it felt like her whole body was on fire.

She cried out.

"Beautiful," he muttered. His hands were still on her, his arms still around her, but he was lightly coaxing her. Easing her down, instead of building her up. "Again."

"No," she said. "This time with you. Please."

Joe slid his hands out of her clothing. Then he reached around her to the cabinet drawer under the sink and pulled out a strip of three condoms.

"Is that going to be enough?" The words she thought were only in her head apparently popped out of her mouth, as well.

Joe chuckled behind her and bent down to kiss her neck, directly on the spot where he'd bitten her.

"It's going to be enough for this morning, sweetheart." He led her out of the bathroom to his bedroom.

This time she wasn't thinking about decorative pillows and furniture. He sat on the bed and tossed the condoms aside. Then he brought her to stand between his legs. He lifted her shirt, and she helped him by raising her arms so he could tug it off. Then he pushed her pants down her legs until she kicked them away.

"Are you warm enough?" he said, looking at her breasts as if he was studying a piece of art.

"Are you kidding?"

He smiled and then leaned forward to kiss the spot between her breasts. He cupped her buttocks and brought her closer even as he slipped a nipple into his mouth. Vivian let her head fall back on her shoulders and tried not to come again. She didn't want an end to this. She wanted the extraordinary feelings to last and last.

He was using his mouth and his hands on her. Finding every piece of skin, everywhere she could feel. And she realized she wanted that for herself, too. She needed to touch him and see him.

She cupped his head in her hands and forced him to look at her.

"My turn," she told him.

He shook his head. "I'm not done with you yet. I need my mouth here." His fingers slid up and inside her, and she swallowed another gasp.

"You're not playing fair."

He put both hands around her waist and pulled her down onto the bed, situating her where he wanted her with her back and butt on the mattress, her legs dangling over the side. He knelt between them.

She'd never let anyone do this to her. She'd always found the act too intimate, but it seemed right to allow Joe to touch her this way. When she felt the press of his tongue between her soaked pussy lips, it was more than just pleasure. It was as if she'd finally come home. She could feel the sobs building in her chest, and she couldn't stop them. Didn't really want to. This was how much she felt.

"Vivian," Joe said as he stood leaning over her. "What? Talk to me."

But she couldn't. Her shoulders were shaking, and the tears were running down the sides of her face. She threw her arm over her eyes so he wouldn't see, but he had to know.

She heard the rustling of his clothes as he stripped, the tearing of the condom package, and nodded. She tried to reach for him.

"Yes, Joe. Please. Please."

He didn't hesitate. He pushed between her legs and slid deep.

"Ahhh."

That was it. That was what she needed. Him deep inside her. He pulled her arm away from her eyes and pinned down her hands on each side of her head with his own.

"Look at me, Vivian. Open your eyes."

She did and it almost destroyed her. Because it was him, naked and on top of her. Him inside her, connecting their two bodies. Him pounding between her legs.

Everything she had ever felt for him was there in her chest, and it felt so heavy. Every ounce of desire he'd ever felt for her was there in his eyes. The way he nearly grimaced each time he thrust as if the pleasure of it was too much to take.

"Damn it," he said as he held himself still inside her. "I can't… I'm not going to…"

Vivian felt like a fertile goddess in that moment. As if the power of her allure was too much for the mighty Joe Hunt. She lifted her legs around his ass and squeezed, and it was enough to send her over the edge again.

Enough for him to give a few quick snaps of his hips, and then he was groaning above her like a man who was being tortured instead of pleasured. He dropped on her like a dead weight, but she didn't mind. The feeling of his furred chest against her breasts, of his hips still pressed tight against her, keeping his heavy cock deep inside her, was magnificent.

Funny, but the sobbing had quickly subsided and now all she felt was tenderness. He released her hands at some point, and she found herself running her fingers through his hair, rubbing small circles on his temple, massaging the back of his neck. Anything that would make him feel good. That was what she wanted to give him.

He lifted his head then and looked at her. Needing to see for himself she was no longer in tears, she guessed. Carefully, he pulled himself away from her and walked to the bathroom. She admired the view of his strong back and narrow hips and tight ass.

She admired the view even better coming back. His penis was semihard, and she craved the feeling of having him between her legs again. Like now that they were separated, there was something missing from her body.

"I think you're right," she muttered. "I'm not sure I remember my name."

He looked down at her still lying on the bed, her legs still dangling over the side, and placed his hand in the center of her chest. Then he seemed to shake off whatever it was he'd been thinking.

"That wasn't much of a ride, babe. I was a little…"

"Needy?"

"Desperate. Next time will be better."

Oh, good. Interesting to know there was something beyond perfection. He pulled the covers down one side of the bed and had her get in. Then he followed and spooned himself around her.

He snuggled his nose under her ear, and she felt surrounded by him. It was lovely. "Give me a few minutes to snooze. You can take a catnap, too."

Right, she wasn't going to sleep. Forget the fact that she had already slept six hours, something of a miracle for her. Her mind was racing. She and Joe had had sex. Ten years of foreplay hadn't disappointed. Not that she minded being held while he slept. It felt as good as it had when they were on the couch together. Total security. Complete safety.

Funny, though—for having gotten as much

sleep as she had, she actually felt a little drowsy. She supposed two orgasms and a crying jag could do that to a woman.

"Sleep, Viv," he muttered again into her ear.

She was about to tell him there was no way that could happen when instead she shut her eyes and felt herself dozing off again.

JOE GOT OUT of the shower and pulled a towel from the rack. He looked in the mirror and saw one very well-laid dude looking back at him. He'd left Vivian in bed because miraculously after their third round she'd fallen back asleep in his arms.

Apparently, he was the cure for her insomnia. Either that or he'd physically wrecked her. The second time he'd kissed her awake, rolled her over onto her stomach and slid into her from behind. He felt like he could pound inside her for hours, but after her second orgasm that round had squeezed his dick so hard, he'd been helpless.

Then he'd made her ride him, and that had been the hottest thing he'd ever seen in his life. Vivian Bennett, her long hair loose down her back, her eyes closed, her back arched. Coming undone on top of him while he watched. No fantasy he'd ever had compared to it.

He wrapped the towel around his waist and checked the cabinet drawer. Those had been his last three condoms. Which meant he was going to have to go out to get more.

He thought about leaving now. He could hit the drugstore at the corner, then stop at the bakery. They had the best coffee and these cream doughnuts she would go ape for. Vivian had the worst sweet tooth...

Joe shook his head. What the hell was he thinking? Damn it, this was exactly what he was afraid of. He wasn't going anywhere without Vivian. He wasn't leaving her unprotected even if he could assume her stalker had no idea where she was right now. No chances. Not until this was resolved.

Her safety had to be his number one priority and his dick was going to have to take a back seat.

Back in his bedroom, she was still sprawled out on her stomach unmoving. He dropped the towel, thinking he would crawl back into bed with her and when she woke they would go together to get breakfast and supplies.

Heck, maybe that was the answer to her

problem. He'd keep her in his apartment indefinitely, while they screwed their brains out, until her stalker got bored and gave up on her.

Then he heard a loud pounding coming from the living room. A really loud pounding.

"That was fast," he muttered to himself.

Quickly finding his flannel bottoms, he threw them on and picked up his T-shirt, pulling it over his head as he made his way to the living room. He thought about grabbing his gun out of the safe in his closet, but it didn't take a genius private investigator to figure out who was pounding on his door at eight o'clock in the morning.

No, it wasn't Vivian's stalker. It was someone infinitely more threatening to their relationship.

The pounding continued, joined by shouting. "Joe Hunt, you bastard, open this door."

Joe took a deep breath and removed the dead bolt lock. He really wished he'd had his coffee before having to deal with the former president of the United States. He pulled the door open, and there was Alan Bennett with his arm raised.

Typical, the man was impeccably dressed in gray slacks and a dark navy sweater. No

jeans and Henley for this guy. Joe wondered
if he'd come directly from the airport, which
would have meant he looked this dapper after
a fourteen-hour flight from Beijing.

Given that there were two agents behind
him, it seemed likely. It also seemed pretty
likely that upon hearing the news of Joe and
Vivian's reunion from Carl, he would have
gone directly to Vivian's place to confront her.

Joe could only imagine what had gone
through President Bennett's mind when he
realized that his daughter wasn't at home.

"Where is she?"

"Good to see you again, sir."

"Where. Is. Vivian?"

Joe knew that voice all right. It was his
presidential, do-not-stand-in-my-way voice.
Alan Bennett convinced a lot of congressman to do his bidding with that voice. But
Joe wasn't having it.

"Sleeping."

That seemed to startle him. "Vivian doesn't
sleep."

Joe shrugged. "What can I tell you? I've got
a very comfortable bed."

President Bennett was practically snarling.
Then he pushed Joe aside as if he was going

to go to his bedroom and drag her out of bed. Since Joe knew she was naked, he wasn't about to let that happen. He grabbed the man above his elbow to stop him. As soon as he did, the two agents who had been just outside the door barged in.

Joe immediately released the president and held his hands in the air.

"I'm not a threat, guys. But, President Bennett, trust me, you do not want to go back there right now. She's not…decent."

Alan turned on him then, a look of fury on his face unlike any Joe had ever seen. And he'd seen this man when Joe had to tell him he'd lost his daughter to a kidnapper.

"You can hit me, but it's not going to change anything."

"You are not going to hit him, Daddy!" Vivian, obviously having been woken by the ruckus, had managed to pull on her pajamas. But her lips were swollen from the kissing and the biting, and she had red splotches along her neck where his beard had scratched her.

There was absolutely no getting around what Joe had been doing with Vivian Bennett for hours before her daddy's arrival.

"I'm going to kill you."

Joe looked over his shoulder at the two agents behind him. "Did you hear that, guys? That was him threatening me, not the other way around."

President Bennett walked up to his daughter, who Joe noticed had lifted her chin about three inches.

"Vivian, get your things and come home with me now."

Joe thought about intervening. He was not about to let him bully her out of Joe's life. But he realized if there was going to be any kind of future between him and Vivian, she would have to figure this part out herself. Her father was a big part of her life, and he wasn't going away.

Very calmly, she said, "No."

"I have no time for your stubbornness. I just got off a flight from China. I'm exhausted and in desperate need of a shower. Now let's go."

"Daddy, if you're exhausted you should go home and rest. In fact, I have no idea what you're doing here in the first place."

"What I'm doing here? No less than two people have told me that my daughter was seen in the company of…him," Alan said, pointing at Joe. As if saying his name was too painful. "A man I hoped never to see again. I show up at your place only to realize you're not there and have to ask myself where else you might be. Trust me when I tell you how wrong I wanted to be. Now get your things."

"I'm sorry. Joe is helping track down the person who might have sent those letters…"

"That's what I have the Secret Service doing! You don't need him."

"But I want him."

"Looks like she's already had him," muttered one agent to the other. Both Alan and Joe shot them deadly looks.

"This is madness. You're going through some kind of…episode…because of these letters."

"She's not going through a damn episode," Joe said.

The president turned on Joe again, and this time Vivian stepped around him. She gave Joe one of her own deadly glares that was actually pretty convincing.

"Stay out of this, Joe," she told him, then turned to face her father. "Joe's correct. I'm not having an episode. I made a perfectly sound decision to hire someone competent to both protect me and investigate the letters.

Someone who had a particular knowledge of this case. Someone I trust."

"How can you trust him? Him of all people in this world after what he did to you."

Vivian closed her eyes. "I have told you this a hundred times and you just won't listen. What happened that night was not his fault."

"That's not true." The president and Joe had responded exactly the same way.

Vivian took another deep breath. Joe had to give her credit, she was holding her own against the old man. As intimidating as he was, she wasn't backing down.

"As for our personal…relationship… Quite frankly, that is none of your business."

"You. With Joe Hunt. None of my business?"

Joe thought steam was going to come out of the old man's ears.

"No," she said very clearly. "It's none of your business. Now, if you don't mind, I would like a shower and a cup of coffee. I'll see you Friday at the Horsham event, and any progress we make on the letters, I'll call to fill you in."

Then she took a bold step and raised up on her toes to give him a kiss on his cheek.

"Welcome back from China."

Alan Bennett remained silent, but he must have sensed this was a losing battle. She wasn't leaving, and it wasn't as if he could force her out of the apartment. He turned to glare at Joe again, but Joe was unfazed. There was nothing the old man could do to him. Outside having his old buddies at the CIA put out a hit on him.

Joe was pretty sure it wouldn't come to that. Mostly sure.

"This isn't over," the president growled at him.

"I know."

"If you let anything happen to her…"

"I won't," Joe snapped. Then he looked the older man in the eyes and said the truest thing he'd ever said. "I swear on my life I'm not going to let anyone hurt her ever again."

"I'll hold you to that. Gentlemen, let's go."

President Bennett and the two agents left the apartment, and Joe bolted the door. Then he looked at Vivian and smiled.

"All things considered, I don't think that went so bad."

She huffed and then left to take her shower. Without anything else to do, Joe followed her, taking his shirt off as he did. They might be out of condoms but there were other fun, shower-friendly activities he might be able to talk her into. Things they could do with their mouths.

And he did.

CHAPTER ELEVEN

VIVIAN BIT INTO her doughnut as they got onto the highway headed toward Maryland. Sweet cream filled her mouth, and she groaned. "Oh man, that's good."

"Yeah. I knew you would like those doughnuts."

Because he knew she had an unhinged sweet tooth. The sweeter the better. He used to tease her about it relentlessly when she would only ever eat the icing off any cake or cupcake.

He knew she would like these doughnuts because he knew her. Or at least thought he did. Now that they had had sex, he probably thought he knew everything about her.

"You know, I've changed, too. In the past ten years. There are things you don't know about me."

She wasn't exactly sure why it was important to her he know that, but she felt especially vulnerable with him this morning. Adding a little mystery might create some space between them. Space she feared she needed as she was quickly growing accustomed to having Joe back in her life.

Too quickly.

Joe glanced over at her and laughed. "Vivian, if there's something fundamentally different about you, I'll eat the bag that doughnut came in."

She squirmed in her seat. "Okay, maybe nothing fundamentally different, but you can't assume you know everything about me."

"I don't."

Satisfied by that answer, Vivian glanced out the window at the cars moving by. She thought about where they were going, and she dreaded it. Having to face McGraw's children was at the least going to be awkward, and at the most painful. Most likely for all of them. Unless, of course, one of them was tormenting her. Then they would probably enjoy her discomfort.

Thinking about them and her reaction to seeing them, she couldn't help think about what her father had said this morning. That she was having an episode related to the letters. Some post-traumatic stress reaction that had sent her running back to Joe.

Which led her to his bed.

Memories of what she and Joe had done together made her squirm in her seat for an entirely different reason. It was like she could still feel him inside her. At the time he had overwhelmed her. Now, trying to look at it objectively, she wondered if her emotions weren't exaggerated.

"What if he's right?"

"About what?" He didn't bother to ask who *he* was, she noticed.

"About why this happened," Vivian said, waving her hand back and forth between them as if he might not understand. "What if both of us were just reacting to the past? Doing it because we wanted to know what it would have been like."

"I considered that," he said.

Which, of course, upset her and annoyed her.

"You did?"

"Sure. That first time, when I was inside you, I thought maybe I've been waiting all this time just to know what it felt like. Then by the fourth time, when you had your mouth wrapped around my cock in the shower, I pretty much knew it wasn't a one-time thing."

Vivian punched his arm. "Jerk."

"Is this when we have the talk?"

"Don't make it sound like I'm being the cli-chéd emotional woman. We do have to talk about this. Yesterday you gave me a list of good reasons why what happened this morn-ing wasn't a good idea."

"I changed my mind."

Exasperated, Vivian hit him in the shoul-der again. "See, that's so like you! You can't just decide something and think that fixes ev-erything."

Joe reached out and grabbed her hand then, entwined his fingers through hers. "I'm not doing this for any reason other than I want you to stop hitting me."

So she reached across the seat and hit him with her other hand, and he had the audacity to laugh.

Laugh, like he was happy. It might have been the first time she'd heard him laugh like that in the past two days. It thrilled her to know she'd caused it.

"Look, Vivian, you're right. There are a lot of reasons why this might be a bad idea.

Maybe it's about the past, but I don't think so. I changed my mind because when I watched you sleeping on my couch, I thought I couldn't not have you. I couldn't live my life on this planet with you and not have you. I didn't have the willpower to stop myself. So I decided to see what it would be like."

"You mean sex?"

"No, but I think we established that was pretty explosive. No, I meant what it would be like to stop fighting myself all the time, stop wanting you and not having you. Like I told you last night, I have no idea what's going to happen tomorrow. So let's not worry about it. Let's do this thing one day at a time."

She looked down at their joined hands, which he'd pressed against his thigh. His thighs were thick and strong and covered with a smattering of dark hair. She longed to see them back between her legs again.

"Do you think it was a one-time thing?" he asked her. "One and done just to see what it would be like for you?"

Since she was staring at his thighs and re-membering how amazing they had felt when her legs were wrapped around them, no, she couldn't imagine not wanting Joe. In fact, she knew with absolute certainty she would want him forever. Only, that wasn't taking it one day at a time. That was wanting everything at once. Which would most likely scare him. Heck, it scared her. Ten years of distance… it should have at least mellowed her feelings. Instead it felt like he was a long-lost lover returned to her.

"Well, you did buy that big box of condoms," she said flippantly. "I would hate for them to go to waste."

"Noticed that, did you?" He smiled at her and wiggled his eyebrows. "I got the jumbo box."

"Okay, so we take this one day at a time."

"And we have lots and lots of sex."

"Plus talking, too. Getting to know each other as the people we are now. That's important, Joe."

He squeezed her hand. "Absolutely. Lots of talking. Between all the crazy hot monkey sex."

She smiled because she couldn't help it. "It was crazy hot."

"Smokin'."

That made Vivian laugh and consider something else. "Funny, it wouldn't have been like that ten years ago. Actually, it probably would have been pretty awful considering I was a virgin when I made my big move. I mean if you had done what you said…about the pounding…it probably would have hurt."

A muscle in his jaw jumped, and she could see she'd upset him. Then she realized it was because he knew who had been her first. Along with the rest of the country.

"Sorry," she muttered. "I shouldn't have brought it up."

"Was that bastard at least gentle with you?"

"He didn't hurt me, if that's what you're asking. I didn't feel much of anything. Certainly not pleasure. But in fairness to him, I don't think I was capable of feeling anything back then. I was this huge empty void."

"Asshole wasn't even making you come and yet he still had sex with you. I swear to God, you're going to have to hold me back when I meet this guy."

That startled her. "Why on earth would you ever meet him?"

"You told him about the name. Which puts him on a very short list of people who knew what McGraw called you. I'm going to need to talk to him at some point."

Vivian groaned again, and not because of a delicious doughnut this time. She looked down at the sweet concoction in her lap, but her appetite was suddenly gone. She put it back in the bag and tucked it away for later when she wasn't having a conversation about how her current lover needed to interrogate her former lover.

Not that she ever considered Nicholas a lover. He'd been…someone to turn to. A distraction. Someone to take her out of her head for a little while. As soon as she realized he was married, she ended it, but by then it had been too late.

Her therapist in Seattle had suggested confronting him at least in a letter. Outlining the damage he'd done when she'd been so vulnerable. Vivian had just wanted to forget the whole incident ever happened.

"Do I have to go with you?"

Joe seemed to consider that. "No. I can leave you with your father."

"Those are my options? Stay with you or my father?"

"I suppose I could trust your safety with Carl and the puppy, too, but beyond that, no."

"They're just letters, Joe."

He glanced over at her, and she knew it was pointless to argue.

"Fine. I get it, but this can't go on indefinitely. You have a business to run, too. I can't be your only client."

"You're my business for now."

He didn't look at her when he said it, his eyes still on the road in front of him, but he'd squeezed her hand and she'd felt it throughout her body. She was under Joe's protection, and nothing was going to compromise that.

With traffic and some of the small-town streets they had to navigate, it took about thirty-five minutes for them to reach their destination—a small ranch house in a blue-collar neighborhood that desperately needed a coat of paint.

There was a white late-model Ford sedan in the driveway.

"I don't know what's worse. The thought of seeing Nicholas again, or having to face Mc-Graw's children for the first time."

Joe looked at the house gravely, and Vivian realized it couldn't be easy for him, either. Though they each knew he'd done the only thing he could to save her, he was still responsible for taking away their only remaining parent.

"Do you know much about them? What happened…after?" Vivian asked.

Maybe it was wrong that she hadn't wanted to know. She remembered at the time that she hadn't wanted to feel sympathy for them. Hadn't wanted to feel as if somehow she was to blame for their situation.

They all got tied up in so much guilt of whose *fault* it was. Vivian's for confronting Joe. Joe's for pushing her away. Vivian's for running. Joe's for letting her go.

Together they swam in it. When in reality there was only one person responsible for everything that happened that night: Harold McGraw.

"I did some preliminary research. Alice McGraw, thirty-four, never married. Works night shifts at a convenience store not too far away. Lives and takes care of presumably her younger brother, George. He's had some minor trouble with the law and served eight months in county for possession of a controlled substance. Couldn't find a place of employment for him currently. They had an older second cousin who took them in after it happened. Not sure why Alice, at twenty-four, wasn't able to act as guardian alone to her younger brother. Instead they both lived with the cousin, Geraldine Hill. She passed a few years back. That's whose house this is."

Neat, tidy facts that really didn't say much at all.

Joe gave Vivian one last hard look. "You're sure you're up for this? I can always take you to your father."

"I'm not sure Daddy is speaking to me right now. Best to give him time to cool off."

It was an excuse, and Joe knew it. The reality was that maybe this was all part of the closure she'd needed for years. Something to finalize it and put it behind her. There were no media, no reporters lurking in the shadows. Just the three of them putting to rest a tragic event that happened ten years ago.

And determining if some new event was controlling the future.

They were still using her SUV, which Joe had proclaimed a sweet ride. They both got out, and she followed him up the broken cement pathway that led to the front door.

Joe rang the doorbell, and Vivian silently prayed no one was home.

Then the door opened and that hope was shattered. Before them stood a woman in her thirties, dressed in a blue jean romper that looked like it was more fit to a girl of nine or ten. Under the romper she wore a white turtleneck with reindeers along the neck. Thick pink hose and white canvas sneakers completed her odd look.

With a face that could have been fifty-four instead of thirty-four for all its hardness.

"Alice McGraw?"

"Who wants to know?"

Joe removed his private investigator license and showed it to her instead of saying his name. Vivian wondered if he thought Alice wouldn't recall the name of the man who shot her father if she read it off a license. She looked up at Vivian.

"I know you," the woman whispered. Then she looked back at Joe. "I know you, too... What are you two doing here? I don't have to talk to you..."

Joe held up his hand as if cutting off what was about to be a hysterical outpouring of hate.

"Alice, you don't. You don't have to talk to us at all, but we have some questions related to some letters Ms. Bennett has been receiving lately, and I would like to talk to you about that. We're hoping you can help us."

"Why would I want to help you? You killed my daddy."

Vivian thought how immature the woman sounded using that word. Especially in the clothes that made her look more like an adolescent than a grown woman. There was something chilling about it. Vivian decided right then she was going to start calling her father by his first name.

From his coat pocket, Joe took out the letter Vivian had given him at that first meeting and showed it to Alice. "Does this name mean anything to you?"

"Huh?" She gasped, then looked at them both as if he'd given her some kind of gift. She smiled, and it was then Vivian knew the girl hadn't mentally survived what had happened to her. Or maybe it had nothing to do with the kidnapping. Maybe growing up with a father like Harold McGraw had affected her. He had been clearly mentally ill.

What if Vivian wasn't his first victim?

"That's what he always used to call me. Please come in."

She opened the door wider, and Vivian exchanged a look with Joe. Wondering if it was safe. He gave a brief nod, as if to say he acknowledged her fear but he wouldn't let anything happen to her.

Trusting him, she followed him inside the aging ranch house. There were only three rooms that she could see, a kitchen and what appeared to be a dining room that opened up into a living room. There was a smattering of fast-food wrappers and crushed beer cans littering the card table in the dining room.

Magazines, books, clothes and other trash took up space along the beat-up wood floors.

If Alice was taking care of her brother in this house, there was little evidence of it.

A threadbare couch and a folding chair were the only places to sit in the living room. The room was dominated by a large flat-screen TV that Vivian, a little sexist in her opinion, assumed was George's contribution to the house.

Alice sat and patted the seat next to her, looking at Vivian expectantly. Cautiously, Vivian sat down, and she realized something else quite startling. She bore a vague resemblance to the woman. Same natural blond hair, same blue eyes, prominent cheeks and chin.

Alice might have been pretty if life had treated her differently.

"That's what he always called me," Alice said in a voice that sounded high-pitched and far away. As if the woman wasn't actually sitting in the room talking with them, but was instead, at least in her head, in another time and place.

"Did he?" Joe prompted.

"All the time. I was his little girl. His little darling. He loved me so much. I wish you hadn't shot him." She looked at Vivian directly then. "You shouldn't trust this man. He kills people."

Joe didn't flinch. He pulled the folding chair a little closer. "Alice, did you have any home movies from when you were a kid?"

Her face turned ugly.

"I did," she said with a scowl. "Then the government people came and took it all away. They took everything."

"What about George, does he live here with you?"

She nodded slowly.

"Does he have a job?"

"Of course he has a job," she snapped. "How else would he take care of me? I tell him all the time, he needs to behave so he can properly take care of me. Sometimes he doesn't listen. Sometimes he gets drunk and says mean things to me, but mostly he's good to me. He says he won't leave me again. Last time was scary."

"Has anyone come by here recently? Asking questions about the past, about your father? A reporter maybe?"

She shook her head. "No. Why would they?"

"Ms. Bennett recently moved back to DC and there was a news feature on her. I was just curious if anyone had asked for your comments about her return to the city."

The girl/woman smiled then, and Vivian thought it was a much older, much more world-weary expression. "No one cares about us. They only ever cared about her. She was the princess. Daddy's little girl. That's what he would say when he saw you on the TV. You were Daddy's little girl."

Vivian felt her skin crawl at the mention of him watching her on television. Knowing it must have begun for him then. His obsession.

"He said that was my problem. Said I had grown up on him too fast. I didn't mean to, I just couldn't stop it. Said he needed to find a new princess. I didn't like you much after that. Not at all."

Vivian glanced over at Joe with a look of desperation. She could feel the panic coming on, and she didn't want to break down in front of this woman. Surely there was nothing else to learn other than Alice McGraw was clearly mentally disturbed.

Joe stood and Vivian quickly followed.

Alice sat there looking at both of them. "Is that all you needed to know about Daddy?"

"Yes. Do you know where your brother works?" Joe asked.

"At the garage a block down from the corner. He gets paid under the table because he's a criminal. But he said he'd behave from now on. Can't leave me again. I'm too little to be left alone like that."

"Thank you for your time, Ms. McGraw."

Vivian was halfway through the house heading for the front door, Joe a step behind her as if to protect her back.

"I love you, Sugarplum."

Vivian froze at the words.

Behind her she could hear Alice, giggling. "That's what he always said before he left me to go to work. I love you, Sugarplum. Did he say that to you, too? Did he? I love you, Sugarplum. I love you, Sugarplum…"

Vivian started running.

CHAPTER TWELVE

JOE PRACTICALLY HAD to sprint after Vivian as she threw herself out the front door. He could hear her panting and knew she was in the midst of a full-blown panic attack. He'd been stupid to bring her with him.

Stupid and selfish—again. He hadn't wanted to turn her over to her father, not after having felt like he'd defeated the old man that morning in what he knew was going to be the first of many fights to come. He also hadn't wanted her out of his sight, having crossed the boundary from past to present. From friend to lover.

He wanted her with him.

However, in that selfishness he'd plunged her back into her past. As if he expected that ten years was long enough to get over being kidnapped and beaten. Mentally and physically tortured for three days.

She doubled over, and he knew she'd reached

that point where she was no longer taking in air, which would send her into another panic. One that might require an ambulance.

Joe didn't hesitate. He scooped her up and carried her to her SUV. He rounded the front and opened the passenger door, setting her down on the seat. She was sheet white and still barely gasping.

He put both his hands on her face and forced her to look at him. Her eyes were glazed over.

"Look at me, Vivian."

When she didn't immediately respond he ordered her.

"Vivian! Now. Look at me." Her eyes blinked and he nodded.

"Okay, now with me, deep breath in." She did as he said. The sound of him taking in air would give her something to focus on.

She tried to mimic him but failed.

"Okay, try again. In. Now out. In. Out. In. Out."

They repeated the exercise over and over until color returned to her cheeks and she started breathing normally again.

"Thank you," she said eventually.

He shook the words away and rested his

forehead against hers. "I'm so sorry, Vivian. I'm so sorry I brought you here."

"It has to be her, doesn't it?" she whispered. "She's not right."

That was evident, and Joe didn't think it had anything to do with the kidnapping. Alice McGraw hadn't recovered from her childhood. From whatever her sick bastard of a father had done to her.

Though it made Joe skeptical that she was even capable of creating and sending those letters. The package of dirt. Alice was a woman trapped in the mind of a child. Joe had a hard time reconciling that with the nature of the letters, which seemed calculated to inflict fear.

He couldn't imagine Alice having that kind of focused intention.

"I don't know, but let's get out of here."

She grabbed his arm. "George. You heard her. He's just down the street. We're here, we should talk to him."

"Are you kidding me? You nearly passed out."

She took a deep breath as if to show him she was fine. "I'm not running away like a scared child."

"Vivian, you have every right to be afraid."

"Of McGraw, not his children. And he's dead. She just...took me off guard. Those words, his words. It brought it back, but I'm fine now."

Joe looked into her eyes. They were steady. Sure.

He nodded and she smiled as if his belief in her strength had been a gift. She fastened her seat belt while he got in the driver's seat. He reached for the button to start the car, then stopped.

"Who did that for you for the past decade?" Joe didn't know why he had asked the question. It would only bring up more of the past. More of her pain. As if he hadn't done enough to hurt her today. Still, it seemed important.

He looked at her then, and she was looking down at her hands.

"Who?" he persisted. "In the hospital, after the rescue, there must have been hundreds of those panic attacks. Who got you through them?"

Joe doubted it was her father. The man had been president at the time, and it wasn't as if he could put his job on hold while he sat by his daughter's bedside. He wouldn't have been there enough to subdue the panic. Hell, Joe wasn't even sure the man knew his daughter had panic attacks.

Vivian lifted her head but didn't look at him. "The nurses mostly. They were very kind."

She wasn't going to ask him, he realized. Of all the things they had talked about she wasn't going to ask him why he left without a word.

Maybe it was better that way. Maybe she didn't have to know everything.

He hadn't lied to her earlier. What happened this morning in his bed wasn't about getting over the past. By the third time he'd buried himself inside her, he knew what they were doing was about the present. The future.

They could have that, he decided. The present and not the past, all the time.

He swallowed. "Okay. You sure you're up for this?"

She nodded, even though he could see her fidgeting with her earring.

"You know, I had forgotten how brave you were."

She looked at him then with an expression of shock. "Are you being funny? I'm the opposite of brave. You just witnessed it."

Joe shook his head. "No, you're wrong. You

were a brave kid. You'd lost your mom, your father was this powerful man, you could have hidden in your room for the eight years he was president and people would have understood, but you didn't. You stood by his side, played the role you were expected to play. Then you held your own for three days with a madman. You could have retreated from the world then, too, but you didn't. Instead you gave an interview."

"Because my father made me," she said.

"But you did it. You handled yourself well. You comforted the country even while you must have been reeling from your ordeal. You don't have to see George. You can wait in the car while I talk to him. Keep the doors locked, keep your cell phone in your hand. You'll be safe enough."

"You don't think I can handle it," she said, and he could see he'd upset her.

"No, I know you can handle it. But I don't want you to have to do it. Please, Vivian, this once, let me actually protect you from pain instead of constantly inflicting it."

She blushed and he knew she was thinking of this morning. When he'd given her anything but pain. He closed his eyes against the memories of how it had felt to have her in his arms. Shaking his head, he focused on the task at hand. Talk to George, keep Vivian safe, get her far away from the McGraw children as soon as possible.

Then he could make love to her again. Pleasure her until she fell soundly asleep in arms.

He started the car and drove the block and a half to the garage. He parked the SUV in front of the gas station and could see a fairly large building behind the pumps with two garage doors. One door was open, a car parked inside. Two men stood in front of it in deep discussion.

"Do you think that's him?"

She was looking at the man in the overalls. Joe thought he looked to be about the right age of midtwenties.

"Stay in the car. Keep it locked. I'll be right back."

"You're being paranoid."

Yep. He probably was. But he knew what it was like to lose her and he never wanted to know that feeling again.

"Do it for me, Viv."

She half smiled. "I guess it goes without saying I would do anything for you."

Joe didn't reply. He wasn't sure what to say. Instead he leaned over and gave her a quick, hard kiss on the mouth. Because he was allowed to. Because he was her lover. Then he got out of the car and locked the door with her inside, and he watched her with glances over his shoulder even as he made his way past the cars in line to get gas and toward the open garage door.

The two men had finished their conversation and the man in the overalls turned to go back inside.

"George McGraw?"

The man stopped and turned. He looked at Joe with suspicion, like he assumed Joe was a cop. "Who wants to know?"

Joe took out his ID. "I'm a private investigator looking into a matter that might be related to your father. Do you know who Vivian Bennett is?"

"That bitch." George, his cheek filled with chewing tobacco, spat as he said it. "Yeah, I know who she is. Got my father killed. Thanks for bringing up such super times."

Joe was grateful he'd left Vivian in the car. He resisted the urge to look over his shoulder to see her, as he didn't want to alert George to her presence. He was also grateful George hadn't clued into the name on the license.

Joe took the letter out of his coat and showed it to him. "You seen this before?"

"No."

"The name, does it mean anything to you?"

George spat on the ground again, this time closer to Joe's feet. "No."

Joe knew this meeting had little to do with getting truthful answers. It was more an assessment of the man. Joe could tell a lot by paying attention to people. George's reaction to the letter, his attitude about the past. All of it screamed defensiveness. If he was guilty of sending the letters, that might be the natural position he would take.

"Has anyone been to your house recently asking about your father? A reporter doing a story, that kind of thing?"

"No. Not that I would talk to any damn reporter. My father is dead and the world treated us like we were freaking lepers. Now I've got a sister who's half-cracked in the head, who *I* have to support, and a house that's falling down around us that I can barely afford. Is that what you want to know?"

Yeah, Joe thought. That was all he wanted to know.

"Your sister…was she always like that?"

George shifted on his feet. He didn't question how Joe knew about his sister's condition. "I guess. I'm ten years younger so I don't really know…how he treated her when she was a kid. I don't think it was good. Loved her too much, I think. All I remember is when he stopped loving her and…turned his attention on someone else, it sort of broke her. Really messed with her head."

Clearly, Joe thought. He felt pity for the girl she'd been and the woman she was now.

"You're wrong to blame Ms. Bennett for your father's death. She had nothing to do with it."

"Good as. Whatever army she brought down on the cabin, he wasn't getting out of there alive."

"I'm sorry for your loss," Joe said. It was a weak effort to atone for the life he took. And while he would never regret pulling the trigger, he did regret making a young man fatherless.

George huffed. "You would be the only one. Are we done here? I don't need my boss seeing me get interrogated. I gotta keep my nose clean."

Joe nodded and turned to walk away. That was when he saw a man near the SUV—and Vivian had rolled down the window for him.

VIVIAN WAS WATCHING as Joe approached the young man in overalls. He had to be George McGraw. She was glad she was far enough away that she couldn't make out his face. She didn't want to see any resemblance to his father.

Joe had probably been right to leave her in the car. There was no reason to confront him when she didn't have to, and no reason why she needed to inflict any more pain on him, either.

He'd suffered the loss of not only a father, but the image of what a father should be. Though given Alice's reaction to her father, maybe that image had already been destroyed.

The knock on the window nearly startled her into another panic attack. Lost in thought, she hadn't seen anyone approach. Turning her head, she recognized Agent Mather and let out her breath. She rolled down the window.

"Hi, Carl."

"I would ask what you're doing here, but I think I know," he said, pointing his chin in Joe's direction.

"He wanted to talk to both of McGraw's children."

"Yep. That's why I'm here. You should have just left this to us, Vivian. I would have handled it."

Vivian bit off a comment about him taking his time. After all, he'd had the letters for weeks and was only now getting around to checking up on McGraw's kids.

"I feel comfortable with Joe."

"Didn't you always," he muttered.

Vivian was about to ask him what that was supposed to mean when Carl leaned in farther.

"I have to say I really am confused by the two of you teaming up. Not for nothing, you destroyed his career. Basically ruined his life. When Agent Thompson suggested talking to Joe about the letters as a suspect, I was like, no way, not Joe Hunt. But I also never would have thought he'd want anything to do with you. Which leads me to thinking, maybe this is what he intended all along."

Vivian felt a chill run through her. "What are you saying, Carl?"

Carl tilted his head, looked away. "I'm just saying be careful, Vivian. Joe Hunt left the Secret Service as a very angry man. You come back into town, letters start showing up at your door and you run to good old Joe just like you used to. What if that's what he wanted? What if all that anger he had isn't gone so much as suppressed right now? What if this has all been a game to him?"

"You're saying Joe's a threat to me," she said tightly. Which was ridiculous.

"I'm saying be careful. Like you said, there are not a lot of people who knew what Mc-Graw used to call you. Joe Hunt is one of them, and you just handed yourself over to him like a lamb to the slaughter."

"I don't believe…"

"Hey! Get the hell away from her."

Carl turned around and Vivian saw Joe's expression change as he recognized him.

"Oh. Hey, Carl."

The older man nodded. "Joe."

"I imagine you're here to talk to George McGraw," Joe said as he approached the car. "I wouldn't bother. He doesn't have anything to do with the letters."

"You seem really sure about that. He's

someone who has reason to be angry with Vivian. At least peripherally for the death of his father."

Vivian didn't miss the subtlety of that statement. She looked at Joe and had to wonder, where *had* the anger gone?

She certainly hadn't felt any residual resentment or anger this morning in his arms. She'd felt pleasured and cherished. Could that have been an act? And if so, to what end? Set her up, get her emotions involved and then… break her heart?

Break her?

It didn't make any sense. Then again, his reasons for making love to her when he'd been adamant they shouldn't just last night were pretty weak.

I changed my mind.

Vivian wished she could have attributed it to his inability to resist her. However, she was far too pragmatic for that. If Joe wanted to resist her, he would have. He didn't take her to bed against his will. He'd done it because he wanted to do it. And she'd let him.

Like a lamb to the slaughter.

The two men were still speaking, but Vivian hadn't been paying attention. However, Alice's name came up.

"Yes. You should talk to her. She's not… right. It's got to be her," Vivian insisted.

Because it couldn't be Joe. If it was Joe and she'd gone so far as to hire her own stalker, then sleep with him, that would make her the biggest fool in the world.

Sort of along the lines of having sex with her married therapist.

"Okay. I'll leave George alone but see what I can get out of Alice," Carl said.

Joe nodded. "Yeah, my gut is saying no, but it couldn't hurt to have a second opinion."

"I'll let you know if I learn anything. You taking her back to her place for now?"

"She's staying with me. I don't like that she got a voice message on her home phone."

Carl nodded like it made sense, but Vivian could almost feel the skepticism. "I see. She's staying with you, then, for how long?"

"For as long as it takes."

"Okay. Well, I'll go talk to Alice, see what we can do to move this along. You headed back to your place now?"

"No, she's got some errands she needs to

run, and since I go where she goes… Well, you know the drill."

Carl flashed a smile. "Yep. I know the drill. I'll let you know my thoughts after I talk to Alice."

"Appreciate it," Joe said.

"It might work better this way," Carl said. "You can watch Vivian. Let me handle the work related to the investigation. This way we're not crossing over each other like we did today."

"We'll see," Joe said enigmatically. Although Vivian knew what he meant. He would do as he damn well pleased and he didn't give a shit what Carl thought.

Carl strolled back to his car while Joe climbed into the driver's seat.

"Why don't you think Alice is responsible for the letters?" Vivian asked as soon as he closed the door.

"Whoever sent you those letters wanted to frighten you. I didn't get the impression Alice had the capacity to formulate a plan, decide what would scare you the most and then put together the letters, the call and the package of dirt. Keep in mind, she considered the term

Sugarplum an endearment. Not something threatening at all."

Vivian dropped her head back on the headrest. She hated it when he made sense. Because if it had been Alice, then it would be easy. It would also be over. Vivian could never be frightened of Alice. A hundred letters could come and it wouldn't bother Vivian in the least. Not when she understood how sick the poor woman was.

"Carl might have a different opinion," she said, more to hold on to some hope it really would be over.

"He might. I'll keep an open mind."

"Joe?"

"Yep?"

"Where did all of your anger toward me go?"

He looked at her sharply. "Where the hell is that coming from?"

"You must be angrier than you're letting on. I destroyed your career. You said it at the bar. I ruined your life. Yet you let me hire you. You didn't let me fire you. You made love to me with such passion but…still, some part of you must be so angry with me for what I did."

"I thought we had moved beyond this," he said tightly.

"Have we? You tell me. You had to have hated me…"

He turned to her, his eyes filled with the anger she accused him of feeling.

"I *never* hated you," he snapped. "Never."

"But you must have been angry."

Joe closed his eyes and then laughed softly. "Anger doesn't begin to cover what I felt. I was furious with fate, McGraw, your father… and yes, you. But the person I was always angriest at was me. Trust me, Vivian, I never hated you."

Certainly not enough to send her threatening letters and then swoop in to rescue her in some twisted game of revenge.

Vivian didn't push further because she already knew.

Joe would never hurt her.

"Ready for some Christmas shopping?" she said, changing the subject.

He groaned, and she smiled at his pain.

"It will be fun."

"Can I pick out a gift for your father?" he asked her. "I'm thinking of something warm and fuzzy…like maybe a tarantula. They sell those, right?"

Vivian sighed. Someday she was going to need to lock Joe and her father in a room together so they could come to terms with each other. She only hoped they both survived the experience.

"Or do you think he's more of a poisonous snake guy?"

"Drive, Joe," Vivian growled.

"Yes, ma'am."

And he did.

CHAPTER THIRTEEN

"You've got to be kidding me with all of this," Joe groaned as he lugged the bags Vivian couldn't carry up to his apartment. He had to give her credit, though—she was hauling as much of a load as he was.

He'd never have thought anyone could buy so much stuff.

"It's Christmas," she insisted.

"I have four siblings and six nieces and nephews between them, and I've never bought so much stuff in my life."

"It's not *stuff*. It's cool presents and you're just mad because you know none of it is for you, which is entirely your fault for not giving me any time alone to shop for you. Except, of course, for the lovely new decorative pillow I found. It's going to look great on your couch. But since you don't understand the concept of decorative pillows, I can't really call it a gift."

Joe ignored the weird feeling in his gut over

the idea of Vivian buying him presents. Yes, they were lovers now, but presents took that to a whole other level. And it also raised the very daunting question of whether he should buy her a present in return.

Instead he focused on the reality of their situation. "That's my job. To not leave you alone. Remember? Bodyguard. Body. Guard."

"Well, you do it very well." Vivian looked at both of them. "We should have taken all of this back to my place. It's never going to fit in your apartment."

"My apartment is not that small. It will fit," he grumbled, moving around her to open the door. He unlocked it and pushed it open. They made their way inside and dropped the bags on the floor. Instantly, Joe felt the hair on the back of his neck go up.

He stilled and looked around the place.

"What?" she asked, seeing him frozen near the door.

"Nothing… I just…" He couldn't put a name to it, but something felt off. Maybe the way the lock turned when he opened it. The room in front of him was as neat as he'd left it; the couch, chair and TV all looked the same. Nothing had been moved or shifted.

Maybe it was paranoia. But paranoia was a state he'd existed in for three years when he'd been a federal agent.

"Nothing," he said again. They stacked the presents in the hall closet, which fortunately was empty except for another coat and a pair of boots.

When they were done, he headed to the kitchen for a beer. "I figure we can order in tonight since you've seen my cooking repertoire already."

"Sounds good. I'm starved. Shopping always does that to me."

"I don't remember you being a big shopper back in the day."

"I wasn't. No money."

Tuition only. It was all her father offered and all Vivian would accept. The rest she had to earn. He remembered respecting both President Bennett and Vivian for that. The truth was, he had respected Alan Bennett a lot, for many different reasons.

Up until the moment he'd stopped respecting him.

Joe opened the fridge and grabbed a beer. He'd also picked up a bottle of wine for Viv, which he put in the freezer to chill.

"The menus are in that drawer over there," he said when she came into the kitchen. She'd taken off her coat and put her hair up.

She looked…at home. It struck him how right that felt when it should have been the opposite. She hadn't been part of his life, his very solitary life, for ten years and yet now she was here and it seemed easy.

Too easy. Or maybe his concern was how fast it was all happening.

"This one? With the paper sticking out?" Vivian opened the drawer and Joe turned to tell her it was the one next to it. Except she was pulling out magazines he didn't recognize.

"Town and Home?" She laughed. "Really? From the man who until today didn't own a throw pillow. I can't believe…"

She stopped as he watched her flip through the pages. The whole scene in front of him was finally making sense with what he'd felt earlier.

He could see as she turned the pages the cuts in the magazine. Spaces where there had once been letters.

Her face was ash white when she turned

back to him. "There's an *S* missing from Santa. And a *P* missing from pole."

"Vivian…"

"Why do you have a magazine stuffed in a drawer with letters cut out from it…? Oh my God. He was right…"

"Who was right?" Joe wanted to know. Someone had done this. Someone had planted this magazine in his home.

"Tell me!"

Joe took a deep breath. "Vivian, I need you to listen to me and think. I've never seen that magazine before in my life. I didn't cut out letters from it. I certainly didn't create notes to terrorize you. Someone wants you to stop trusting me. Most likely so they can separate us, but that's not going to happen."

Vivian looked at the magazine in her hands. "It makes sense. You said it yourself about Jefferson. Send me notes, frighten me, then come swooping in for the rescue. But why? What's your endgame? What kind of revenge would satisfy you? Or did what happen this morning already do that?"

"I have no endgame, and that doesn't make sense. Remember, you came to me."

Vivian looked at him, and Joe could see her

doubts. "Because of what was in those letters, and you could have predicted I would do that. Or if you didn't, then maybe I handed you a better opportunity. Instead of terrorizing me, you got to fu—"

"Don't say it," he snapped, cutting her off. "Don't you dare say that's what this morning was about. You need to hear me. Someone broke in here, someone planted that magazine. When I walked through the door earlier I sensed it. Something was off, I just couldn't put my finger on it."

"Why?"

"I told you. They want to separate us. Two reasons for that. Either to make you more vulnerable or to remove me from your life. If it's the latter, then I'm about ninety percent certain that someone was your father. Or at least someone working for him."

"Daddy wouldn't... Dad wouldn't do that," Vivian argued. "He's not the monster you think he is."

Not a monster. Just a very angry father. Who hated his daughter's current lover. "No, but he's the person who most wants you as far away from me as possible. Doing something like this, making you doubt me. It's the most expedient way of accomplishing that. That's not my magazine, Vivian. I did not send you those letters. I have been by your side every second for the last two days. You tell me when I would have been able to deliver a package of dirt to your office."

Vivian set the magazine down on the counter. Carefully, as if it might explode in her hands.

He could see her wavering. Trying to look at the facts as they were, not as they seemed to be. "Maybe it would make more sense for me to stay with my father until all this is over."

"No!" Joe barked. Not when he'd only just gotten her back in his life. Not when he'd finally gotten her in his bed. Then softer, he said. "Don't let him win. Please, baby, don't give up on me."

Vivian shook her head. "I'm telling you my father didn't do this. Sneaky is not his style. He'll rant and shout and pound his fists, but he wouldn't do this."

"Vivian, look at me. Look at me!"

She did, and it almost broke his heart. She'd never looked at him like she was now. Like she didn't believe in him. He hadn't realized how much her belief in him meant, and how it made him feel to have it back after all these years.

He wasn't going to lose it.

"Okay, let's take a step back. You wanted to know what my endgame was. What is it, then? What do you think it might be?"

"To hurt me," she whispered.

"Physically?" It killed him to think she might believe he would hurt a woman. "Last night you fell asleep on top of me over there on that couch. I could have hurt you at any point I wanted."

She closed her eyes. "Not like that. You wouldn't hurt me physically. I know that."

It was something. "But you think I would hurt you emotionally?"

"You have. You did. In the past."

There was no denying it, but she wasn't the only one who suffered. "I think we know now that sword cut both ways. Finish it off, then. Why now? Why after ten years would I do this?"

"Because I ruined your life. You said it yourself!"

Joe looked away from her then. He wasn't going to convince her. The evidence was clearly stacked against him. He *had* told her that. He'd meant it, too, but not in the way she understood it. And he had hurt her in the past.

The only thing in his favor had been her faith in him, and apparently a magazine with a few missing letters was enough to shake that foundation.

"I didn't send you the letters," he repeated. "I didn't have sex with you for any reason other than I wanted to. Because I've always wanted to. And the reality is you have someone invested enough in doing this to you, which means they would commit a crime to plant evidence. The stakes just got raised. Go get your stuff. I'll take you to your father."

Vivian walked by him, and Joe felt as if she'd sucker punched him. He thought of what this meant to their future. As long as she was with her father, Alan Bennett wouldn't let Joe anywhere near her. A more devout Capulet had never existed. Even if Joe found who was doing this and handed the person to Carl Mather in handcuffs, he doubted President Bennett's opinion of him would change.

If Vivian left him over this, they were finished. And while Joe had enough pride not to fight with someone who was calling him a liar, he knew one thing for certain.

He wasn't done with Vivian. This couldn't end now. Not this way. Not because someone had orchestrated it.

Joe moved back to the apartment door to check for any physical signs of the break-in. It was a dead bolt. Nothing fancy. He was on the third floor of a locked building, and he had a weapon. Beyond that, other than his TV and laptop, there was nothing in the place worth stealing.

Yet anyone with a basic understanding of locks could get through it.

George was a mechanic, so he must know his way around tools. Alice? It seemed unlikely, but he couldn't rule out that he'd spoken to both of them today and several hours later he had a drawer filled with magazines.

His address wasn't easy to find online, as he'd taken precautions to list himself privately, but anyone with a talent for digging could find the information.

Certainly someone with government contacts would have no problem.

He understood Vivian's point about her father's style, but what if someone on his staff had decided to take initiative? Break Joe and Vivian up first, take credit for it with the former president later? He'd seen up-and-coming politicos do worse things to get ahead.

Then there was Jefferson Caldwell. Someone who certainly didn't like the idea of them being together. Although he doubted the guy had the balls for something like this.

Vivian came back into the room, but she wasn't wearing her coat or carrying her bag.

Hope surged.

"Breaking in to plant magazines isn't my father's style. I know this. Deep in my gut I know this. But cutting up magazines to send threatening letters isn't your style, either. I know this, too."

Joe nodded and felt a wave of satisfaction fill him. The look was back. The one that said "I'm counting on you to let nothing hurt me."

"I'm sorry I doubted you," she whispered.

Joe opened his arms, and in a second she was in them. He wrapped her up tight and thought if only he'd done this back then. If only he'd kept her permanently in the shelter of his arms. Maybe nothing bad would have happened to her.

"I'm going to find the person who is doing this," he promised her.

"It has to be one of his kids," she mumbled against his chest. "We were just there this morning."

He lifted her face to his.

"I'm going to dig a little deeper. With both of them. I might have underestimated George."

He bent and kissed her. To re-create the intimacy of the morning, to stake his claim a little deeper, to see if she would respond as willingly as she had before.

He'd almost lost her.

He pulled away and looked at her again. Belief and desire. Both for him. It was his favorite combination.

"I've got to call Carl."

Vivian winced. "Why?"

"You know why. He's got to investigate the scene, take the evidence."

Vivian nodded. "Right. Sorry. It's been a long day."

AN HOUR LATER there was a knock on Joe's door. Vivian waited on the couch as Joe got up.

"We seem to keep running into each other," Carl announced as Joe opened the door.

"Crazy, isn't it?" Joe quipped.

"Hi, Vivian." Carl waved to her.

"Hey, Carl." She didn't want to see the expression on the agent's face, the one that said I told you so, so she fussed in the kitchen making coffee.

"You have something you want to show me?" Carl said.

Joe had vaguely explained the situation when he called Mather, saying only that he had new evidence that should be checked out.

He walked Carl to the kitchen where he'd left the magazines untouched since Vivian had paged through them. He used a pen to turn the pages and showed Carl the cutout letters.

Carl immediately turned and gazed at Vivian, but she looked away.

Joe laid out his suspicions, and Carl watched him with a quizzical expression. "So you're saying someone broke into your place and planted the magazines."

"Yes."

"I get we worked together for a long time, but people can change. How the hell am I supposed to know these aren't your magazines?"

"I'm turning them over to you. My prints are on file. You run it. Also, you'll want prints on the door to my apartment and downstairs."

"Like you wouldn't have known to wear a pair of gloves."

Joe shrugged. "It's all you have to go on."

"Fine. Let's say I believe you. Why you? All this time Vivian has been the focus. Why go after you? How would this guy even know you two were together?"

"I've been by her side for the last forty-eight hours. Anyone watching her would have seen both of us. It wouldn't have been too difficult to track down my identity. I'm guessing whoever it is wants us not to be together anymore because it would make her more vulnerable."

"Are you sure it would?" Carl asked.

Vivian heard the skepticism in the other agent's question.

"Yes," Joe said definitively, obviously ignoring that skepticism.

"Vivian, are you certain you don't want me to take you to your father?"

"She's not going to her father," Joe told him.

"I'll let that be her call."

"I'm staying with Joe," she said firmly.

She knew that if she went to her father, if she had to tell him about the magazines and questioning whether Joe was behind everything, he would never let Joe get within a mile of her again.

It would be over between them. Finally and irrevocably over, and every cell in her being rejected that concept. Joe was hard. And sometimes he could be cruel. But Joe was not evil. There was evil in those letters. In the phone message. He would protect her from it. She was certain of it.

Carl shrugged. "I don't get you two. Never have and probably never will, but I guess I just have to accept it. Okay. I'll take the magazines now and send a team out to print the doors sometime tomorrow."

"Appreciate it, Carl."

Carl looked at Vivian again. "You know what you're doing?"

"I do," she answered. Definitively.

"Did you talk to Alice?" Joe wanted to know.

Carl nodded. "Like you said, she's freaking out there."

"What time were you with her?"

"Got there around two, was done by two thirty. Two forty latest."

"Which would have given her plenty of

time to drive here and break in," Vivian pointed out.

"That's your theory? Alice saw you together and figured she could make you more afraid if you thought Joe were behind the letters?"

"Possibly," she said.

"You think she's capable of it?" Joe asked Carl.

"I think crazy people are capable of anything they put their crazy minds to. Look at freaking McGraw."

After that, Carl secured the magazines in a plastic evidence bag and left.

Joe shut the door behind him and stared at Vivian. "*Are* you sure you know what you're doing?"

"You're trying to make me doubt myself?"

"I don't want you to have any doubts. But you can see others will have them. If your father is blameless, then when he hears about the magazines—and trust me, he'll hear about them—he'll be back."

"Then I'll explain to him why I'm staying with you. I'll be reasonable."

Joe thought there was nothing reasonable about her decision. She'd changed her mind based on emotion. Emotion she felt for him.

Vivian got off the couch and walked over to him. She wrapped her arms around his waist and squeezed him tight.

He pressed his hand against her cheek and thought again how incredibly beautiful she was. When he looked into her stunning face, he saw, too, that the dark bruises under her eyes were lighter than they'd been a few days ago.

"Come to bed with me?" he asked her.

"Okay. But you know I won't be able to sleep… I mean after. I just don't want you to feel like you have to worry about that. The fact that I've gotten as much sleep as I have in the last few days probably means I'm due for no sleep tonight."

"I won't worry about after. But I'm sure going to pay a whole lot of attention during. Is that okay with you?"

Vivian smiled. "A-OK."

Hours later Joe looked down at Vivian, who was soundly sleeping, her face resting on his chest, her arm draped over his waist. Soft in-and-out breaths he could feel on his skin. The slow up-and-down of her body as her heart beat. The hot touch of her skin against his. All of it, a gift.

After he'd gotten up to get rid of the condom, she'd changed into her pajamas, ready to leave the room. But he'd asked her to stay with him for a little bit. She teased him about being a cuddler, because *cuddle* and *snuggle* weren't two words he used a lot. He'd said he'd just wanted to hold her a little longer, which was something he knew she wouldn't refuse.

Within minutes she was out.

He wanted to shout to everyone to look at what he'd done. He'd made her feel safe again so she could sleep. It made him feel like a god.

Except she wasn't going to be completely safe until he stopped whoever the hell was doing this. Someone who now had gone after him. Someone who liked to play mind games.

Mind games?

Joe considered that and figured it was about time to meet Vivian's infamous psychologist.

He only hoped he could refrain from hitting him when he did.

CHAPTER FOURTEEN

VIVIAN ROLLED OVER on her back and realized something strange. Her brain was waking up. Consciously she understood that, but as she opened her eyes she realized the sun was shining through the windows. Morning. She tried to put back the pieces of last night.

She'd made love with Joe. Then he'd wanted to cuddle—though he refused to use that word. She must have fallen asleep in his arms and now it was morning. Sun-already-up morning. Not 3:00 a.m. in the morning, but actual morning.

It was unthinkable.

She hadn't slept that long since…well, yesterday. This was incredibly outside the norm for her. The bed was empty, but she could hear puttering down the hall and could smell coffee. That was probably what woke her up. She might have slept even longer.

Getting out of bed, she made her way to the

bathroom and then into the kitchen where Joe had poured her a cup of coffee.

"Good morning," he said with a bit of a smirk.

"Good morning," she mumbled.

She felt vaguely out of sorts. Almost as if her body and brain were conditioned to run on no more than three hours of sleep and all the extra snoozing was making her loopy.

"How did you sleep?" he asked, clearly wanting to remind her that on two occasions she had said she wouldn't sleep, yet on two occasions with him she had. The pattern wasn't lost on her.

"You know that's more sleep than I've gotten the past month. Stop being so smug."

"Hey, I'm only pointing out that if you let me nail you nightly we might be able to overcome your insomnia altogether."

Vivian scowled at him. "I think what I missed most about you was your romantic side."

He smiled and bent down to give her a kiss. Then she was in his arms and she could feel his hand slide into her pajama bottoms, and she thought that this was very much something she could get used to. Every morning waking up to kisses from Joe. Except then he was pulling away from her.

"We've got appointments we have to get ready for."

She sighed, because she knew what that meant. Thinking about the letters and who might be sending them to her instead of thinking about how…happy she felt.

Because this was happiness. The real thing.

Joe made her happy. With Joe, she had no problem falling asleep. Sure, multiple orgasms were conducive to relaxation, but it was more than that. The reality was she hadn't felt safe in ten years. Not deep-down, it's-okay-to-let-go safe. Not since the night of her kidnapping.

She appreciated the irony of being in the most danger she had been since that night yet finally finding some peace. Because of Joe. Had she known it was going to be like this, she might have tracked him down years ago.

"Let's not go to wherever you are taking us," she said with a pout. "Let's stay in and watch stupid Christmas movies until our eyes glaze over and then have more sex."

He cupped her cheek and brushed his thumb under her eye, where she knew she always sported a prominent pair of dark circles.

It was her worst feature. "They're getting better," he said gently.

"I don't want to go," she whispered.

"I don't, either, but it occurred to me last night that the person doing this likes to play mind games. Mind games, Viv," he repeated.

"Oh no," Vivian groaned, realizing who they were going to see.

"Sorry, baby. I wouldn't be doing my job if I left any string unchecked. He's a string."

"He's a douchebag," Vivian replied.

They had talked with McGraw's children, which left only one other person alive who knew what the term *Sugarplum* meant in context. A person who once was in the profession of using mind games to manipulate people.

It made sense to follow up with him, but she didn't have to like it.

"No argument from me, but it has to be done. What's he like in general? Other than being a manipulative scumbag who would take advantage of a patient and trauma victim."

"You mean other than that?"

"I'm looking for details, Vivian."

She pulled out of his arms because in some ways it seemed wrong to be talking about an ex-lover while her current one held her. She took her coffee and sat in his chair cross-legged.

"You know what this chair could really use?" she said, avoiding the topic.

"More throw pillows. I mean, look at what the one you bought yesterday has done for the entire room."

She looked over at the couch and saw it. The colorful pillow now sitting innocuously on the black sofa did in fact cheer up the room. More affecting was the fact he'd taken it out of the bag and actually put it there this morning. Because he knew it was important to her, or because he liked showing off a gift she gave him. Either reason touched her heart.

"It's perfect. And more would be transformative."

"Yep. Got that. Lots of pillows. Now spill it."

Vivian sighed. How to explain Nicholas in a way Joe would understand?

"He was very authoritative. Not bossy like you, but it always felt like he was in charge of our session. It wasn't me talking about my fears, rather it was him taking me to a place he wanted me to go. It wasn't until I saw a therapist in Seattle that I could understand the difference. I'm sure he was under a tremendous amount of pressure from my father to *fix* me as soon as possible, but that's not how it's supposed to work."

"Viv," Joe growled. "Do not defend this guy to me."

"I'm not. Only trying to explain what might have motivated him. I was not in good shape… after. It upset my father tremendously. Especially since there was nothing he could do about it. My father doesn't like it when things are not in his control."

JOE HAD TO fight his instant reaction to her words. Listening to her talk about this was not easy. Not because it reminded him of the past and his role in it, but because she'd been the one who had been kidnapped and abused. She'd been the one who suffered at the hands of a madman.

Yet she seemed almost guilty for upsetting her father. Felt bad for a therapist who had been pressured into fixing her.

Upset enough that she felt the need to apologize to Joe. Joe, who was responsible for allowing it to happen in the first place.

It was crazy, but it was also Vivian. Giving instead of taking. Thinking she was a coward because she had panic attacks and insomnia instead of realizing how brave and amazing she was for building a fulfilling life after all the tragedy.

"You did nothing wrong," he muttered.

"I know that," she said.

"Do you?"

"Of course. The only person to blame for what happened is Harold McGraw."

Joe doubted that, though now he found himself less worried about the time and being late for an appointment.

"Do you need to take a shower before we go?"

"I know. As soon as I finish my coffee."

"No," he said, walking over to her. He reached out his hand. "How about now, with me?"

"With you?"

"Yes."

"But you look like you already had your shower."

"I'm just there to wash you," he said. To give to her. To make her the center of every ounce of attention he had in him to give.

Vivian put the coffee cup down and took his hand. "Did you change your mind again?"

"I did."

She followed him down the short hallway to the bathroom. He turned the water on to let it heat up, and when she reached for her T-shirt, he stalled her hands.

"I'm taking care of you now. Follow my lead, okay?"

"Joe…what are you…?"

He pressed a finger against her lips. "I'm taking care of you. That means I undress you."

He found the elastic waistband of her pajama bottoms and pushed them down. He tapped her right ankle and she stepped out of them, then her left and she did the same. Then she held her hands up while he pulled the T-shirt up and over her head.

For a minute he just stared down at her body, taking in her beauty. He brushed the hard tip of her nipple with this thumb and reveled in her small gasp of pleasure. It was heady knowing that she was his to please now. That he could tease her, and please her and make her come.

Because she was his. He took off his shirt and stripped out of his jeans. He lifted her up and placed her in the shower, under the hot spray of water.

Then he stepped in with her and found the shampoo, squeezing some out into his palm. He lathered it and then gently cupped her head with his fingers. It was something he'd never done before, never thought about doing, but there was something about the act that seemed incredibly intimate. Like she was a precious thing he could wash and care for.

"I'm not an invalid," she said, sensing what he was doing.

Joe rubbed the shampoo into her hair and then pulled her under the spray. "Didn't say that you were. Like this, though. A lot. Let me take care of you, will you?"

He rubbed some of her fancy conditioner in next. Then it was the body wash, only instead of using a washcloth, he used his hands. Rubbing the soap into her skin. Along her arms, over her belly, into her breasts, before turning her so that her back was to him.

He kneaded her shoulders and then squeezed more of the silky soap against her back. She let out another gasp as the cool liquid hit her water-warmed skin.

Slow circles with his hand over her shoulders, down her back and then around to her stomach, up to her breasts where her nipples were still tight with arousal. Down to her perfect ass, which he couldn't help but enjoy, startling her with a quick slap.

"Joe," she moaned, her head falling forward.

He knew what she wanted, where she probably most wanted his hands, but he wasn't done yet. He needed her to fully understand this was about her. He got down on his knees and paid tribute to her legs.

He stroked her thighs and knees and ankles. He noticed how different points he touched caused her to tense and moan. Only when he was satisfied that he'd touched every part of her, learned everything he could about her body, did he stand and press his chest against her back.

He circled an arm around her stomach, his palm flat against her sex. His cock had been hard the second he touched her. Now it throbbed against her ass cheeks.

"Joe, please…"

"Please, what?"

"Anything," she cried. "Just please."

He bent her over then, pressing her hands

to the tile, and he smiled grimly as she spread her legs for him. One heavy thrust and he was inside her. The heat and wetness blew circuits in his mind. Except he knew what he was doing. Knew he'd done this without a condom.

"Joe?"

There was no concern in her voice because she knew he would never do anything that would hurt her. He loved knowing that. "It's okay. I'm clean as a whistle, baby. I promise."

"It's not that... I am, too...but I'm not on the pill or anything."

His head dropped against her shoulder and he kissed her. In her ear he whispered, "I'll take care of you. Trust me."

He pushed inside deeper, and she groaned his name.

"Trust me," he repeated even as he started to move with urgency.

"Ahhh," she cried and slapped her hands against the tile wall.

The hot water poured over them as he held her hips steady and pounded deep and hard inside her.

This was what it would feel like, he realized, if they wanted to get pregnant. With no barrier between them. A hope to start a family. Children. Vivian and his children. A wave of emotion overcame him, and he had to grit his teeth to stop himself from coming.

Knowing he was on the edge, he moved his hand between her legs, sliding his fingers against her as she pushed back against him in time with this thrusts.

"You need to come now, Vivian," he growled against her neck.

"Oh, Joe… I'm so close… Harder, harder."

He gave her what she asked for even though it cost him all of his control. "Now, Vivian!"

He felt her tighten around him. Heard her cry out his name and knew in that moment she belonged entirely to him. It took all of his effort to leave her body, but she trusted him to do that. So he did, spilling his seed on the tile floor instead of deep inside her. Which, crazily, he so badly wanted to do despite the consequences.

Together they leaned against the tile wall, breathing heavily. Joe held her tight against his chest. Ten damn years, he thought. What he'd been missing all this time, if he had known… "I should have never let you go," he said into her neck, and he wasn't talking about that night at the party.

She tilted her head to give him better access, and he noticed that she didn't disagree with him this time. Possibly because she was too relaxed to fight, or possibly because she understood he wasn't talking about the party.

Eventually he recovered and rinsed her off again. Then he pulled her against him, turned the water off, got out and lifted her out of the shower.

"Joe, I can walk," she said against his neck, although she didn't move to get out of his arms.

"Damn. Then I didn't do it right."

She chuckled then, and he set her down on her feet. He took the towel off the rack and dried her as thoroughly as he had washed her. His precious gift.

"I'm not fragile. Seriously, I won't break."

No she hadn't broken. Not matter what she'd experienced. And she had suffered a lot. Through it all, she was still his Viv and he...

Joe stopped himself before he could finish the thought. He wasn't ready to think that far ahead.

Really? Hadn't you been thinking about children when you were buried deep inside her?

"We need to go," he said, suddenly wanting to get away from his own thoughts.

"Okay. I actually think I can do this now," Vivian said as she wrapped a towel around herself, about to head back to the bedroom.

He caught her hand before she could leave. "It's not that I think you're fragile. I don't think that all. I just like taking care of you. That's all."

She smiled and leaned up on her toes to kiss his cheek. "I'm not going to lie, Joe. I do like being taken care of by you. You do it *really* well."

He let her go and decided he wouldn't disagree with her. He'd messed up in the past, but that didn't mean he couldn't change everything for her going forward.

They had the stalker business they needed to get through, but then maybe they could actually have a new start. A real chance at a future together despite everything that had happened.

Inwardly, Joe groaned. How the hell was he going to convince her father he was the best man for his daughter?

Give him a granddaughter...

It was definitely an idea.

CHAPTER FIFTEEN

JOE WAS JUST coming out of the bedroom dressed for the second time that day when he heard a knock on the door. Carl had mentioned that agents would be by at some point to take prints. Joe would let them in to have at it while he and Vivian kept the appointment with the douche bag.

Joe's lips twisted at the thought of the elegant Vivian using such descriptive language.

He opened the door and was surprised to find the puppy, aka Agent Thompson, there instead.

"Mather sent you to take prints? Seems a little demeaning, kid."

The kid frowned. "I'm not here to take prints. We have support staff coming by later this afternoon to do that."

"He fill you in on what's happening?"

"You mean the magazines of a suspicious

nature that somehow were found in your apartment? Yep, he filled me in."

Joe thought if he snarled it might intimidate the kid, but the truth was he didn't care. Vivian believed him, and that was all that mattered.

"Why are you here, then?"

Agent Thompson reached into his pocket and pulled out a photo. He handed it to Joe.

"After Carl told me about the magazines, I realized I now had an ally in my own particular suspicions. So I started looking back a little further in time before the notes started. What you are looking at is a security image from a camera on the street where Ms. Bennett's business is located. Does the person in the photo look familiar?"

Joe glanced at the picture. It was from a considerable distance. Probably the end of the street. The picture was grainy at best. But in it he saw a man of a certain height, standing outside approximately where Vivian's Creations store door would be.

Joe checked the date and time of the photo.

"No," he lied.

He hated to do it, but there was nothing about the picture that was definitive. Just general height and size that matched his. If the puppy had a shot of his face, they would be having this conversation in his office.

The kid was taking a shot. A good one— he wasn't wrong. That *was* Joe in the photo. The day he'd gone to see her shop. The day he'd stood outside as a thousand things raced through his mind.

The day he'd turned and left and come up with another plan instead.

"You don't mind if I show Ms. Bennett?"

"Show me what?" Vivian came down the short hallway looking, in Joe's opinion, more beautiful than she'd been the day she found him at Dom's.

Sex and sleep were an awesome combination for her. One Joe planned to provide more of in the days and weeks to come.

"Vivian, this is the puppy. Sorry, Agent Mark Thompson. Agent Thompson, this is Ms. Bennett."

"Please, call me Vivian." Vivian reached her hand out and the agent shook it. With a little look of awe on his face.

Joe handed her the picture. "Can you tell who is in that picture?"

She looked at it. "No, it looks like a man, but I can't see his face at all. What is this?"

"It was a picture taken outside your store several weeks ago. Soon after you opened, actually."

"Okay."

"In the footage the person stands outside the door for some time, then eventually walks away," Agent Thompson added.

Vivian looked at Joe. "I'm not getting it."

"The man is about my height. Same build. The puppy is making an argument it was me."

Vivian scrunched up her face. "You can't even see a face. That's ridiculous. Look, Agent Thompson, I'm going to lay this out for you. There is no way that Joe is responsible for those letters. None. This is not me being naive or foolish. I'm telling you what I know. And a grainy photo of some man standing outside my door is not going to shake that conviction."

"Yes, ma'am. I just thought… Well, again, it's up to us to follow every lead. I'll leave you to your day."

Vivian handed him the photo back and Joe shut the door behind him after he left.

"Crazy. If I wasn't going to believe you

were behind the magazines, what made them think some fuzzy picture would make me doubt you? I'm going to freshen my lip gloss."

Yes, Joe thought. It was pretty crazy that he'd lied to a federal agent in the middle of an investigation. Crazier still that she trusted him implicitly.

But if he had confessed it was him, then he would have to explain it to Vivian. He needed more time with her, time for her to see them for what they were today, for what they could be in the future, before he could do that.

It wasn't too much to ask for, he thought. Just more time.

JOE PULLED HER SUV into the parking lot and turned off the ignition. Vivian felt the muscles in her stomach tighten. Which somehow Joe sensed.

"I told you, you don't have to do this. I can drop you off with your father. Now that I know you believe me, I'm not worried about him keeping you away from me. He can take you to the charity event tonight and I'll meet you there."

Vivian shook her head. "This isn't like facing the McGraw children. This was my mistake. I need to own up to that. And if he is connected to this in any way, I want to tell him myself to go to hell."

"It *wasn't* your mistake," Joe growled. "He abused your trust. It's why he doesn't have a practice anymore. Shrinks are not allowed to mess with their patients."

Vivian put her hand on his arm. "I love that you want to protect me, but I still screwed up. You have to let me own that."

Joe didn't look as if he agreed, but he said nothing more.

"All right. Let's do this. I hope it is him so we can put him in jail."

"I don't think that's likely," Vivian replied. It didn't make sense to her that after all this time Nicholas would suddenly want to inflict any kind of harm on her. "I still think Alice is responsible. I can't get her voice out of my head saying...that."

"I did a little more digging this morning. While you were sleeping..."

She rolled her eyes. "Yes, Joe. You've made your point.

He chuckled. "Anyway she has spent time in a mental health facility. Twice. Once as a teenager and then again not long after her father's death."

"How did you get hold of her medical records?"

Joe lifted an eyebrow.

"Right," Vivian muttered. "Nothing is protected when you have friends who have access to that information."

"I'm going to do whatever I have to, Vivian. Which means calling in every debt I have out there. I'm only telling you about Alice because I agree with you. Given her medical history and from what we've both seen, we know she's unstable enough to send those letters. I put a call into Bill to see if he's gotten anywhere with the recordings. But for now we have to at least talk to the douchebag if for no other reason than to eliminate him."

Vivian nodded.

They got out of the car and made their way up the sidewalk to the community college's main entrance.

Joe had given Vivian a basic rundown as they drove out to the school. Nicholas had lost his practice soon after his wife exposed his sexual conduct with a patient. Then she'd reported his behavior to the Virginia state licensing board, which had revoked his license. Left with only a PhD, an alimony payment that ate up all his savings and a devastated reputation, he'd taken the job as an instructor at the small school in suburban Takoma Park, Maryland.

Psychology 101.

Vivian tried not to take any pleasure in his fall from grace. What she had told Joe was true. It was her mistake. She slept with a man she didn't love for the worst reasons. To hurt Joe. To feel something other than the emptiness she had been feeling at the time. Possibly in some demented way to hurt her father, too, or to show him she wasn't the perfect little princess who would blindly take his orders anymore.

It didn't matter. She'd done it. She'd been subjected to a nation's condemnation, and she'd accepted that.

However, as much as it had been her mistake, she could admit now that it had also been Nicholas's. Whatever fate delivered as a result of that was his to own, as well.

Joe stopped and asked at the help desk situated just behind the main entrance for a map of the campus and a listing of the classes being offered. A helpful freshman coed obliged, and Vivian couldn't help but think how young the girl looked.

Young and innocent. Waiting to really start her life as an adult. The way Vivian must have looked back in college before the kidnapping.

Joe was seven years older than she was. It was easy now to see how any feelings he must have had for her would have been a struggle for him. Because unlike Nicholas, Joe was a man of honor and integrity who never would have used his position of authority to his advantage.

How naive she'd been to think any relationship they might have would have been on equal footing. She was a college student trying to find her way in life, while he'd already been a mature adult with a career and a home. Their power balance would have been completely lopsided if they had attempted an actual romantic relationship. Joe, of course, having all of the power, while she worshipped and adored him.

Maybe they had each needed these ten years for her to really grow up so that she could take on the force that was Joe Hunt on her own two feet.

He came back to her, shoving the map in his back pocket. "It's down the hall and to the right. A class should just be letting out."

Vivian nodded and then looked over at the coed again. "Was I ever that young?"

Joe smiled. "You were younger."

"That's not possible."

"Honey, your father covered you in Bubble Wrap the day your mother died. His goal in life was to make sure you never experienced hardship or pain in any fashion. When I met you, you had none of the typical experiences a teenage girl might have had, but you could pull off socializing with diplomats and presidents at a state dinner. It was…weird. Let's face it, you were weird."

Vivian couldn't argue. No previous boyfriends. No previous real girlfriends, either. Tutors instead of classrooms. No catfights, no jealousy, no having to stand up to a bully. Other than her father.

By that point, Joe had graduated from West Point, had served in the military as an officer. He'd had any number of girlfriends. Yes, they would have been completely out of balance.

Vivian shook her head. "There never would have been an *us*. Back then. I mean even if you had kissed me and lifted me onto that bathroom sink and…"

"Pounded into you until you forgot your own name," Joe finished, remembering what he'd told her about how he'd felt.

"Yes. Even if you had done that…it wouldn't have been easy."

Joe turned to her and cupped her cheek in his palm. "Babe, it would have been impossible. We would have had to keep it secret, which wouldn't have sat well with either of us. You were not going to lie to your father like that. I wouldn't have liked lying to my superiors or my family, either. Our only other option would have been to go public, in which case I certainly would have lost my job. So that's me, with no job and a girlfriend in college who I can't even come close to supporting."

"You thought about it," she whispered, looking into his eyes. "You actually considered the possibilities and our options."

He dropped his hand then and turned away from her. Clearly not comfortable admitting any of that.

"Come on," he said instead and with his chin directed her to follow him. "Let's get this over with."

Vivian was still processing what that meant when a door opened and a rush of students poured out into the hall. They stood back, giving the kids a chance to exit, then walked inside the very normal-looking classroom.

Rows of desks and small podium in the center of the room.

And Nicholas. Who currently looked like he was flirting with a slim blonde twenty-something student. Vivian supposed some things never changed. He still had that attractive intellectual quality. A boyishly handsome face, with round wire glasses, a pointed chin and deep brown eyes that seemed to see right through a person. His brown hair was scruffy around his face, and Vivian could see gray mixed through it now. She did the math and realized he was in his fifties.

She'd wondered how she would feel seeing him again. She knew how emotional it had been to see Joe that first time. She'd been nervous, excited, curious. All emotions hitting her simultaneously until she thought she would come out of her skin.

With Nicholas, there was none of that. Still, she was feeling something.

"Dr. Rossi," Joe said sharply enough to get

Nicholas's attention away from the blonde. "If I could have a minute of your time?"

"And you are?" Nicholas asked. Clearly he hadn't seen Vivian, as she was standing behind Joe.

She moved out from around him and tried to fake a small smile. "He's here with me, Nicholas."

"Vivian," he whispered, then seemed to shake himself out of the past. "Long time."

Not long enough, Vivian realized. She had expected awkwardness, but she hadn't expected anger—hers. Because looking at the blonde who was gazing up at him like he was some kind of supergenius, that was what Vivian felt.

All these years she thought she took her share of the blame rightfully. But seeing him ten years later doing the same thing with a girl who was less than half his age made her realize how truly flawed a man he was. So flawed, and yet he made a living telling people how to fix their own problems. She wanted to call him out as a hypocrite but knew that would get them nowhere. Vivian smothered the anger and got down to the business at hand.

"Yes. I wouldn't be bothering you if it

wasn't important. If Joe and I could ask you a few questions. It's related to the kidnapping."

"Gretchen, I'll catch up with you," he told the girl, who pouted childishly before grabbing her schoolbag and leaving.

Joe watched her walk by and heard the door close behind her. "Seriously, dude, how young do you have to go to get a woman to buy into you?"

Nicholas flinched but then quickly recovered. "Young enough. I'll ask again, who are you?"

"I'm Joe Hunt and I'm investigating..."

"Joe Hunt?" Nicholas sputtered. "The actual Joe Hunt? Are you serious, Vivian? Did I not get through to you at all?"

"No," Joe snarled. "You didn't get through to her, but you sure as hell got into her, didn't you? Wasn't that your primary objective? Bang the first daughter so you could feel really important?"

Nicholas stiffened. "You don't know what you're talking about. Vivian and I cared about each other. Tell him."

Vivian felt nauseated. "Is that what you told yourself? That I cared about you so it was okay to do what you did?"

Nicholas sighed. "Oh, here we go. The innocent act. I forgot how well you played it. Like that day I told you about my wife finding out about us. You acted so shocked and appalled, as if you hadn't known all along I was married."

"I was shocked. And appalled," Vivian snapped back. "How the hell would I have known that? You didn't wear a ring. There were no pictures around the office. The only time we…did it was during a session…so it wasn't like you were bringing me home where I might, oh, I don't know, meet your wife. What you did was so disgusting on so many levels it took me years of therapy to get over being treated by *you*!"

Nicholas huffed, stuffing papers into his leather satchel. "I forgot. The ever-virginal Vivian. Always the victim. Always needing some kind of daddy figure to come in and save the day. Until your shining knight over here, the one you had convinced yourself you were in love with, abandoned you and you fell apart. Which left you with me as a surrogate. Tell yourself all you want I was to blame. There were two of us in that office."

"Yes, and one of you was supposed to be

offering help. The other was a kidnapping victim," Joe pointed out.

Nicholas tilted his head. "Why are you here? Obviously not to skip down memory lane. It's been ten years, and quite frankly it's a chapter in my life I would rather forget. No offense, Vivian."

Joe removed the letter from inside his leather jacket and set it down on the podium in front of Nicholas.

"What's this supposed to be?"

"Vivian has been receiving threatening letters like this."

"And what's that got to do with me?"

"Sugarplum," Vivian said, hating the sound of those words on her lips. "It was what he called me. I told you that during our sessions."

Nicholas looked down at the letter again as if he hadn't understood the ramifications of the endearment.

He nodded his head. "Yes, I remember now. Again, what has this got to do with me?"

Joe shrugged and looked around the small community school classroom. "Not exactly a thriving practice. Not even a four-year private college. I assume this was the best you could do after losing your license and reputation."

Nicholas's jaw tightened. Vivian thought now there was really nothing attractive about him. He looked exactly like he was, just a small, flawed man.

"Yes."

"Seems to me a man might hold a grudge. You were making well over six figures. I can't imagine a community college comes close to that in salary."

"It doesn't," he snapped. "Your point?"

"You're one of the few people who knew the name McGraw had used with Vivian. She was on television a few months ago. A piece about her returning to DC and her expanding interior design business. Maybe you see that piece on the news and resent the fact that she's done well for herself while you…haven't."

Nicholas chuckled and removed his glasses, reaching inside his satchel for a cloth to wipe the lenses. Vivian remembered vividly when he used to do that during a session. Always looking at her so thoughtfully, but when the glasses came off and he rubbed the bridge of his nose, she knew the session would change into something else.

He put them back on now. "I did not create that note and send it to Vivian. I did not see the piece on the news. I watch very little television. I prefer to read. I have not thought about Vivian Bennett in ten years, not since that horrible press conference. Sorry, Vivian, if that's harsh for you to hear, but I had other concerns. The breakup of my marriage, the loss of my practice and the fact that I was suddenly thrust into a national scandal because my wife was a vindictive bitch. Trust me when I say this, if there was ever anyone I would consider terrorizing, it would be my ex-wife and not Vivian."

Joe seemed to accept that answer. "Has anyone been around in the last few months asking questions about that time?"

"No."

"Any reporter?"

"No. Nothing like that."

"I assume you kept notes during your sessions."

"Of course," Nicholas huffed.

"Where do you keep those notes?" Joe wanted to know.

Nicholas smirked. "All notes related to my sessions with Vivian were turned over to the Secret Service ten years ago."

"What?" Vivian charged. "The things I said

in those sessions, that was private. How could you?"

"Vivian, when the president of the United States says turn over the notes, you do it. Besides, it wasn't as if I was writing down what you said. I was writing down my thoughts about what you said."

"Would you have written the word *Sugarplum* in those notes?" Joe asked him.

"Honestly, I can't recall. I might have. I knew you didn't like the endearment. You didn't like that he considered you a loved one. It made him human to you when all you wanted was to see him as a monster. Plus there was the juxtaposition of using the name while he was physically hurting you. You struggled with that. So yes, I might have written it down in my notes as a reminder to explore that."

"You didn't keep a copy of those notes?" Joe asked.

Nicholas shook his head. "They were in notebooks. All handwritten. And like I said, they were all turned over at her father's request. My guess is he wanted to make sure none of what I had written was ever seen again by anyone. I wouldn't be surprised if he had them destroyed."

Joe looked at Vivian, but she shrugged. "He never said anything about it to me. But we weren't exactly on great terms back then, what with me being an adulteress and everything."

Nicholas smirked. "Still having daddy issues? Not really all that surprising considering the role he played in your life. Also not surprising you ran back to your dear Joe at the first sign of trouble. Which has to make *you* wonder."

Nicholas pointed at Joe.

"Wonder what?"

"What if Vivian never got over her obsession with you? Maybe coming home and realizing you were still in the area triggered all those feelings of needing to be rescued. Saved by her very own knight in shining armor."

"What are you saying?" Vivian asked, not exactly thrilled with the idea she was *obsessed* with Joe. It wasn't a healthy word.

"What if she's sending those letters to herself?"

Vivian rolled her eyes. "Give me a break."

"You were the victim of kidnapping. You

suffered abuse at the hands of your captor, and you were abandoned by the man you thought was supposed to protect you. All of that could have broken what was a fragile constitution to start with, leading you to create these letters as a way of getting back what you lost. Was there any other scenario in which you two might have reunited?"

Vivian didn't care for that beat of silence that followed his questions. Sadly, he was right. She didn't know if she ever would have had a reason to contact Joe if it hadn't been for the letters.

"That's what I thought," Nicholas said smugly. "Very unlikely."

"You have no idea what you're talking about..." Vivian started.

"Vivian," Joe said, cutting her off. He reached for her hand. "It's not worth it. We're done here."

"Rings a little too true, doesn't it, Joe?" Nicholas taunted. "I mean, you have to know mentally she wasn't the strongest of women."

Joe turned back to him then and got up in the older man's face. "You want to know how strong she is? She survived the death of her mother, she grew up alone in the fishbowl that is the White House. She survived her over-bearing father, she survived McGraw, she survived me and most of all, you sick bastard, she survived what you did to her. Because of you she had to listen as the nation collectively called her a whore. That's not fragile in my book. That's strength. What a truly crappy therapist you must have been if you can't see something that obvious."

Nicholas had no reply and again Joe turned, taking Vivian's hand and leading her, practically at a sprint, out of the classroom. He didn't say anything until they reached the car, and once they did he slammed his hand against the steering wheel several times in a way she knew must hurt.

Knowing that he was hurting himself in lieu of hurting Nicholas.

Her poor steering wheel was taking a lot of abuse lately at the hands of Joe Hunt.

Vivian reached over to him. "Stop," she said gently. "He's not worth it. Remember?"

"That slimeball douchebag!"

Vivian couldn't help but smile. She couldn't remember a time when she'd seen Joe lose his cool—except after their first kiss. He always kept his emotions in check.

Well, maybe not always. The night he found her after he killed McGraw he'd been shaking so hard another agent had had to come in and cut off the ropes. Funny how she had forgotten that until now.

"Why your father didn't confront that bastard. I will never forgive him for that! He promised me…he freaking promised."

"Promised you what?"

Joe didn't answer, he just shook his head.

"Don't say that you won't forgive him." Vivian ran a hand over his arm to soothe him. "I can't have the two men in my life at war with each other."

He looked at her, and she could see the anger leaving him.

"Do you think I became unhinged in the last ten years and sent those letters to myself so I could get your attention?" Vivian asked, a smile playing around her lips.

Nicholas really was quite ridiculous.

"No."

She smiled fully. No hesitation, no uncertainty. It wasn't the craziest scenario if she had in fact become unhinged, but he didn't doubt her. Not even a little bit.

"Thank you." She leaned over and kissed

him. A second later she felt his hand on the back of her neck and then he was really kissing her, and she wondered if there would be room for her to crawl into his lap. But he pulled away.

"Not here," he said roughly, and she thought he might have been thinking the same thing.

"Home?" she asked, meaning his apartment. That was probably strange, too. After two nights with him, it already felt like home.

"Home," he agreed and looked almost maniacal as he started the car and drove them back into the city.

CHAPTER SIXTEEN

"How do I look? And keep in mind there is only one real answer to that."

Joe was fidgeting with his tie when Vivian came down the short hallway into the living room. She was wearing a black strapless gown that hugged her body as if it had been made for her, which in all likelihood it probably had been. Her hair was swept up in a sophisticated bun she'd done herself. And her jewelry, all presents on various occasions from her father, not overdone, made her look like a woman of both class and money.

"You're stunning," he said honestly. Too good for him, quite frankly, tuxedo or no.

She took the ends of his bow tie. "Here, I can help. Go sit down so I can get behind you."

He sat on the kitchen chair and she tied the tie quickly and efficiently without cutting off his air supply. Something she had probably done for her father countless times.

Her father, who would be at the charity event tonight. Her father, who hated him. Her father, who let the slimeball douche bag therapist hurt her without any consequences.

And Joe somehow needed to convince him he was worthy of his daughter.

Despite the fact he had once upon a time let her get kidnapped by an evil monster.

This was probably going to be an eventful night.

"Okay, stand up and let me see if it's straight."

Joe obeyed and was patient as she tugged at the bow until she determined it was perfect. Then she took a step back and smiled. It was if she'd wrapped her very own Christmas present and was pleased with herself.

"Well?" he said, turning from side to side. "Do I pass muster?"

She smiled seductively and nodded. "Considering I'm sitting here wondering which Joe I like the best—Tuxedo Joe or Naked Joe—I would say that's a big fat yes."

Joe chuckled and then caught her hand, pulling her close. He bent down and whis-

pered in her ear, "Naked Joe. You can feel my
skin, touch my ass, stroke my cock."

She shuddered in his arms. "That's true.
Naked Joe is a lot of fun. But Tuxedo Joe
looks so handsome. Like James Bond handsome, which is really hard to resist."

"I will make a compromise. You get Tuxedo
Joe for the next few hours and then when we
get back here, Naked Joe comes out to play."

She kissed his cheek. "Okay, I'll invite
Naked Vivian and we can have lots of fun."

Joe felt heat flood him, and if he didn't
know that her father was most likely already
at the party waiting for them, he might have
tried to convince her they could be a little late.
Instead he nodded toward his living room.

"See that couch over there? Take a long look
at it because when I get you home I'm not
going to be able to wait to take you to my bed.
I'm going to strip you of this gown and bend
you over the arm of that couch and take you
from behind in your high heels and diamonds."

Her eyes lit up and he knew she was feeling it, too. "Promises, promises."

He reached around and slapped her lightly on
the ass. "Let's go," he said. "Daddy is waiting."

"Promise me you'll be civil."

"I promise I won't make a scene."

Joe had every intention of having a conversation with her father privately. He would feel safe enough leaving Vivian in the company of a roomful of politicos to make that happen. Whether or not it remained civil depended on President Bennett and his ability to accept Joe's presence in Vivian's life.

"Good enough. Okay, let's do this."

Joe couldn't help but think it felt more like they were walking into a battle rather than a party.

THE PARTY ITSELF was held at the Willard Inter-Continental, one the oldest and most upscale hotels in Washington. They left the car with the valet, and Joe escorted Vivian inside the swanky hotel, his hand at her back. They dropped off their coats and headed into the crowded ballroom.

He'd forgotten what this was like. The pomp and circumstance. The fake smiles. The air kisses. And the diamonds. The freaking diamonds glittering on the women.

Glancing down at Vivian, he found it strange to see her so at ease in this world. He knew her to be mostly shy around people, prone to the occasional panic attack, but in this world she still moved like she belonged. Shoulders back, chin high, gracious smile firmly in place.

That was Alan Bennett's doing, as well. He had raised her to feel at home among these people. No wonder he wanted to marry her off to an up-and-coming congressman. He probably thought she longed to be back among the politically powerful, in a world where she fit. A world where he didn't.

Then she bumped into his side. "I really don't miss this at all."

"Really?"

She looked up at him quizzically. "You think I like these kind of parties?"

"I think you look like you belong. I think I don't."

She patted his chest. "I think you underestimate yourself. You're the only person of substance in this room. The only one whose expression matches what he's actually thinking. If I belong, it's because my father rounded off all the edges of this particular square and then pushed it through the circle."

"Speaking of squares…" Joe drawled.

"Vivian!"

Jefferson Caldwell approached them both, and Joe tried to contain his scowl as the man bent to kiss Vivian on the cheek. She didn't give the congressman an air kiss in return.

"Hunt," he acknowledged.

"Jeff," Joe returned.

"Still acting as Vivian's body man, I see."

"As we haven't identified the person responsible for sending her those letters, yes. Of course, even if we had identified that person, I would still be here as her date. So for tonight I'm both."

The man flinched. "I see." He turned to Vivian. "I can't say I'm not disappointed. I had hopes for us."

"I'm sorry, Jefferson," she said gently. "But really, you don't know me all that well. I think you would find me to be a poor politician's partner."

"I don't think anyone could call you *poor* at anything." Jefferson nodded to Hunt. "I'll see you around this evening. Maybe I can have a dance as consolation."

"That would be nice. Joe doesn't dance."

"Excellent."

He walked away from them, shaking hands

and kissing cheeks with a host of people along the way.

"That went well," Vivian murmured. "Not too awkward."

"He's definitely a politician."

"Jefferson was the warm-up. Now comes the main event. Here *he* is."

Joe braced himself as President Alan Bennett made his way through the crowd of people like a shark who was tracking down blood in the water.

He stopped in front of them, his fierce scowl taking over the space as if he commanded the air around them.

He turned to his daughter with a slight bow of the head. "Vivian, you look beautiful. Really quite stunning tonight."

"Thank you, Dad."

He gave her a strange look and then bent down to kiss her cheek.

"I take it you've made no progress in finding the person who is terrorizing my daughter."

"I've ruled some people out. Your boy Jefferson being one of them."

"Joe!" Vivian squeaked. "He didn't mean it. He had some ridiculous idea Jefferson was using the letters as a way to get closer to me. I told him it was impossible."

In doing a more thorough background check on the congressman, he agreed the guy didn't fit the profile. He was squeaky-clean, which was hard to do for a politician. After talking to a few people who knew him well, there was no sense he would play games to get the attention of a woman. It seemed Jefferson could have his pick of eligible women in this town.

"Jefferson Caldwell is a fine man and a courageous politician," the former president snarled at Joe. "Do you honestly believe I would encourage a relationship for my daughter with someone so completely disturbed?"

"No." Which was why Joe felt comfortable handing her over to the congressman now.

"Vivian, why don't you go have that dance with Jefferson? I would like to have a word with your father in private."

"Joe," she warned. "You promised."

"No scene, just a conversation. I think we need to get a few things straight between us. Don't you agree, Mr. President?"

Alan Bennett stared at Joe while he spoke to his daughter. "Vivian, is it your intention to have this…person in your life against my deepest wishes?"

"Oh, Dad, please let's not do this."

"And since when did you start calling me *Dad*?"

"Since I realized how silly 'Daddy' sounds coming from a thirty-year-old woman."

President Bennett frowned. "I rather liked it. It made me feel like you would always be my little girl."

Vivian leaned up and kissed his cheek. "I'll always be your daughter, but I'm not a little girl anymore. You have to stop treating me like I am one. Joe is a part of my life and, yes, I hope he's going to be a part of my future once this letter stuff is behind us."

President Bennett looked at the two of them. "Then I agree we should talk. I'm sure we can find a private conference room not in use."

Joe turned to Vivian. "Find Caldwell. Dance with him, drink with him. Stay by his side no matter what. Hell, make him think he's got a chance if that's what you have to do."

Vivian nodded. "Can I make out with him?"

Joe glared at her. "I'm serious, Vivian."

"You're always serious, Joe."

"I'm not leaving this room until you're on the dance floor with him."

Vivian took a deep breath, as if struggling for patience. "Do you and my father seriously need to do this here and now?"

"Yes. You know we do. This is at least neutral territory. Please," he finally added, leading to her downfall. "For me. I won't feel comfortable unless I'm certain you're secure."

"Joe, nothing is going to happen to me in a crowded ballroom. However, I'll go and dance with Jefferson if it makes you feel better."

She walked off and Joe followed her through the room until she approached Jefferson. He led her to the dance floor, and only then did Joe turn to the former president.

"Let's go."

APPARENTLY ALL IT took was a word in the ear of the hotel concierge for the former president to be granted a quiet room complete with a bottle of Scotch and two glasses. Alan Bennett walked to the small bar and poured himself two fingers. He made a gesture with the bottle and the second glass but Joe shook him off.

"I'm driving. And working."

Alan nodded. "Advantages of having a personal driver. So tell me, Hunt, do you think my daughter is in actual danger from whoever is doing this?"

"I don't know. There is something about this I can't put my finger on. Something that doesn't feel right. Alice McGraw clearly has mental health issues…"

"You saw her?"

"Yes. We spoke with both his children."

Alan's stern gaze grew even darker. "You took my daughter to see that monster's children? What in the hell were you thinking?"

"I'm looking for answers," Joe fired back. "And she doesn't leave my sight."

President Bennett's head tilted. "Is that what this is all about for you? Some sort of do-over? You can't fix what happened in the past."

Joe shook off the question. "That isn't what we're here to talk about. I wanted to tell you to your face that you left your daughter to hang out to dry during that damn scandal when you promised me you would look after her. I don't know if I can ever forgive you for that."

Alan Bennett slammed the glass of Scotch down on the bar and marched toward Joe until he was standing directly in front of him.

"Then you need to know something, too. I don't think I'll ever be able to forgive you for losing my daughter to a monster who abused and starved her for three damn days!"

Joe took the force of that anger and laid it out. "That's really it, isn't it? Why you hate me. Because for the first time in your life you knew real fear. That's what you can't forgive. I made you weak, and Alan Bennett isn't made weak."

The former president laughed. A harsh sound in the quiet room. "No, son, I knew fear before. When they tell you your wife is filled with cancer and only has months to live, that's fear. When you have to look into the eyes of your twelve-year-old daughter and tell her that her mommy is sick, that's fear."

Joe flinched. He'd known Vivian's mother had died of cancer, but hearing President Bennett say it suddenly made it real. She'd been so young. Too young to die.

"But you're right," Alan Bennett continued. "Your losing Vivian isn't the only unforgiveable thing you did. It didn't occur to me until weeks later. Watching my daughter, living and breathing, yet still dead inside. It wasn't just the violence of the kidnapping. It was…sadness. Then I recalled your face in the hospital that night. The anguish. You weren't upset you had failed at your job or failed me. You were upset because you failed her."

This time Joe wouldn't flinch, but he felt the punch of those words in his gut.

"You were a twenty-seven-year-old man. She was a student. An assignment. And you fell in love with her. How pathetic is that?"

Joe closed his eyes. He'd never heard the words out loud before. Never even thought them. He'd told himself that he wanted her, that he lusted after her. Never that he…

"Was it how she looked at you? Like you were some kind of hero to her? You should have been a better man. A bigger man. Instead you let yourself get distracted, and it could have cost her her life."

No. He didn't deserve all the blame for what happened after the kidnapping. "You should have let me stay with her in the hospital. I could have helped her. Calmed her. She needed me, and you knew it. You caused that sadness by sending me away."

"What in the hell do you think that would have accomplished? Your sitting by her side, holding her hand. Then what? Do you honestly think the two of you might have had a chance at some kind of relationship?"

"We'll never know."

"No. We won't. And do you honestly think, after everything that's happened between you two, you can make a relationship work now?"

"I don't know," Joe said softly.

"'I don't know' isn't good enough for my daughter!" Alan roared.

Which only served to piss Joe off. "Well, that's too bad, Mr. President, because I am not going anywhere. You forced me out of her life once and I let it happen because I was filled to the eyeballs with guilt over what I had done. Yes, I should have been a bigger man, a better man, but I wasn't. I loved her and then I failed her, and it crushed me. You never had to see what she looked like. Tied to that chair. But that is an image I will never forget! You say you know fear. Well, I know it, too. But that is done and behind us. If I have a chance to make her happy, I'm going to try."

"Happy?" the older man barked. "You *destroyed* her when you left. You didn't have the courage to come back even though you loved her. You were a coward who ran. I might have told you to go, but you weren't man enough to fight for her."

Joe felt a moment of despair. Alan Bennett was right. He'd walked away because he thought it was for the best. He'd walked away because he couldn't stomach his guilt. He'd walked away because part of that guilt was having feelings for her in the first place.

But if he'd loved her—really loved her—then Bennett was right and he had been a coward.

There were so many reasons for her father to hate him. To hate them together as a couple. But if they were going to have a future, he knew some sort of understanding had to be reached here. If Alan Bennett only knew…

"She sleeps with me."

Alan turned away from him in disgust. "Yes, I'm aware you are screwing my daughter. Thanks for the reminder." He picked up his drink from the bar and took a large gulp.

"No, I mean she sleeps. With me she sleeps all night. This morning she didn't wake up until well after nine. Almost ten hours of sleep."

This time President Bennett carefully put the crystal glass down on the bar. He walked over to a brown leather chair and sat heavily. Only then did he look up at Joe.

"She really sleeps?"

"All through the night. Every night she's been with me."

The man closed his eyes and leaned back in the chair. "You can't know how awful it was. When she got out of the hospital she would wander around the White House all night like a ghost. I tried everything, but nothing stilled her. The staff would find her asleep in a chair in some room or another. Twenty minutes here or there. Maybe an hour or two. I knew it was because she lived with fear. Fear I couldn't make go away. You can't know what it's like to be the most powerful man on the earth yet not be able to do a thing to help your daughter. Finally I sent her to that…that…"

"Slimeball douchebag."

Alan Bennett smirked. "Indeed."

"You should have had her back," Joe said. "His wife called her a whore on television. You should have called the woman out for that."

Slowly, Alan nodded. "The irony of it was that scandal seemed to pull her out of her funk. It was like she had this other thing to focus on so she stopped thinking about the kidnapping. Stopped thinking about you. She left the city, headed to the West Coast and made a life for herself. I was so proud of her. So proud that instead of falling victim to it all, the kidnapping, you, the scandal…that she picked herself up and made herself be strong. I don't know if I've ever told her that. How proud she makes me. She really sleeps?"

"Soundly," Joe said.

President Bennett regarded him then. "You're not going to let anything hurt her again."

"No."

"How strange that I find myself believing you."

"I messed up," Joe admitted. "On many different levels. I didn't want to…feel what I felt but it's… I… I couldn't stop… I was…"

"Helpless?" Joe sensed the older man was enjoying his word choice too much. "Weak? Yeah, love can do that to you."

Love. It seemed inconceivable to Joe that he could have felt that strongly back then. Then again, he knew as soon as he heard she was back that he was going to somehow find her.

See her. On the Metro. At a Starbucks. Some accidental meeting.

A feeling that had lasted for ten years had to be pretty damn powerful.

Alan Bennett stood then. "I think we're done here."

"Yes, sir."

"You say everything you needed to say?"

Joe nodded. "Did you?"

President Bennett nodded, as well.

"Are we going to be able to be in the same room together?" Joe asked him. "Christmas is around the corner."

"Keep my daughter safe. Keep my daughter happy. We'll manage."

"One last question," Joe said as they walked to the door of the room. "What do I call you?"

Alan stopped and looked at him. "President Bennett."

"Here I was thinking 'Daddy.' I know how you like it."

The former president's lips quirked. "Alan will do. Now, if you don't mind, I would like to dance with my daughter."

"When you do, look at her eyes. She's not hiding any dark circles. They're nearly gone."

"Make sure it stays that way and we'll do

better than manage. I might even find it in me to like you."

There it was, Joe thought. All he needed to earn Alan's respect was to make his daughter happy. Still, that granddaughter idea wouldn't hurt, either.

"Yes, sir."

CHAPTER SEVENTEEN

VIVIAN WAS DANCING with Jefferson, who really was a lovely dancer, but she kept her eyes on the ballroom entryway. Waiting for Joe or her father to return—or hopefully both men together. Because if they were together it meant the situation hadn't come to blows.

Finally, after several anxious turns around the dance floor, she spotted them. Standing together. Her father looking stern but not angry. Joe looking...determined. She thought that was a good sign. The music ended and she and Jefferson politely applauded the band.

"Another dance?" Jefferson asked hopefully.

Vivian smiled and touched his arm. "Sorry. My father and Joe are back and I need to make sure neither one of them is bleeding from internal wounds."

He nodded. "Listen, Vivian, I just wanted to say... I know you think this was all a setup between me and your father. That my reasons for wanting to date you were for political advantage…ah, heck, the truth was they were at first. Not advantage really, but I thought it might be easier. It's hard dating as a congressman because you have to explain the life to the person you're with. What's expected of them because of who you are. You, well, you understand how that life works."

"I do," she agreed. "But I also know that when I was living in that fishbowl all I wanted to do was get out. While my father can't comprehend not wanting to be a part of that world, I wanted to stay as far away from it as possible. I meant it when I said I would be a horrible political wife, because the first thing I would ask my husband to do would be to not run for office."

Jefferson sighed. "I can't not run."

That made Vivian laugh. "I know. Because you're a politician."

He smiled sheepishly. "I really do like you. It wasn't all about the politics."

"Thank you," she said. "I appreciate that. But I…"

She looked over at Joe, and she could see

he was starting to get impatient. His hand was tapping his thigh, and it wasn't to any music.

"Yeah, I've seen the way you look at him. Figured out pretty quickly I didn't have a shot when I ran into the two of you at the restaurant, but I really hate to lose." He smiled. "Because I'm a politician."

"Am I that obvious?" Vivian wondered, tugging on her earring. Because if she was, she knew how vulnerable that made her.

"Let's say I'm good at reading people."

"That was a very politically correct way of saying yes. Thank you for reminding me I need to work on my poker face."

Jefferson chuckled "If it makes you feel any better, he looks like he wants to end me right now, so it's not one-sided."

"Thanks for the dance, Jefferson."

"Good luck."

Vivian headed toward her father and Joe. It was so easy to spot them. They weren't necessarily the tallest men in the room, but they seemed to take up the most space. Their similarities weren't lost on her. The same sense of honor and righteousness. The same sense of power. The same stubbornness.

Her father wanted her to marry a future

president, but really she wanted to marry a man who was like him as a person, not a president. She wondered if her father and Joe could see the similarities. She doubted either would admit it, if they did.

"I don't see any blood dripping. I'm assuming that's a good thing."

"Come here, Vivian," her father commanded. She obeyed and moved to stand in front of him. He stared down into her face, and she had absolutely no idea what he was looking for. Then he turned to Joe and grunted.

"Anyone want to clue me in?"

"Dance with your father," her father insisted.

Vivian turned to Joe. "I assume you trust me with him."

"Barely."

Her dad grunted again and took her hand.

"I'll be back." She smiled.

Joe nodded, but then her father was leading her out onto the floor. She had no problem following his lead. His ability to make people go in the direction he wanted was his superpower.

"So," she began. "You two talked."

"We talked."

Vivian looked at her father's face for some indication of how that talk went, but she could see he was thinking about something else. Something that was far away.

"Vivian, you know I loved your mother very much, don't you?"

That was the last thing she was expecting. "Of course I do."

"When I found out she was sick…it was a feeling I had never known before. Terror. Absolute terror. Of losing her, of you losing your mother. I was filled with it day in and day out, and there wasn't a single thing I could do about it. The doctor who had given me the news… I despised her. Every time she tried to explain to me what was happening inside Margo's body, all I could think of was that if I hit her she might stop talking."

Vivian gasped. The thought of her father getting violent with anyone was a stretch; let alone with a woman. He was a talker, a negotiator, not a fighter.

"I know. Horrible isn't it? But it's also the truth. Then Margo was gone and I didn't think anything would ever frighten me again because the worst thing that could happen already happened. Until the night Joe Hunt walked into the residence rooms at the White House to tell me you'd been taken. My opinion of him was no different than my opinion of Margo's oncologist, I'm sad to say."

"Oh, Daddy," she said, not able to help falling back into old routines.

"He was there at the hospital."

She almost tripped over her own feet, but her father caught her and smoothly turned in time to the music.

"As soon as they put you in the ambulance, he followed you. He was outside the private room where they were treating you."

This time she did stop dancing. She looked over to where Joe stood, his eyes firmly on her.

"You said he wasn't there. When I asked where he was, you said he hadn't come to the hospital. That he'd been fired and was no doubt packing up his things back at headquarters."

Her father flinched. "I did that because I wanted to bring home to you that you were his assignment. That having been fired from the Secret Service, there was no need for his continued involvement with you. I thought it would help make you understand. The way you called for him… I realized then how you felt about him. I could see you were crushed. But I didn't realize…not until it was too late… how he felt about you."

Vivian nodded. "Joe came to the hospital. To see me. He was there. He didn't just leave me."

Alan shook his head. "I wouldn't let him see you. I wouldn't let him speak to you. I thought it was the best decision for you. Now I realize maybe I wasn't acting in your best interest. Instead I was acting based on my emotions. My fears. Because I was so afraid for three days…so afraid, when I thought I never would be again. I'm sorry, baby, that wasn't fair to you. I suppose it wasn't fair to him either."

Vivian looked at her father. She wanted to tell him that he was right—it wasn't fair. If she'd known that Joe had come for her, if she'd known then that he cared enough to at least be at the hospital with her, she would have known he felt something for her. She would have known that their connection wasn't nothing. That he'd lied to her at the party. That she had been more than an assignment to him no matter what he'd said to her.

She would have known then what she'd only recently learned now. She wasn't crazy.

Adolescent crush. Hero worship. Fantasy-based infatuation.

Or love.

"I can't undo a ten-year-old mistake," her father continued. "Truthfully, I don't know what would have come of it if I had let him through those doors, but it wasn't my call to make and I shouldn't have done it."

"Thank you," Vivian said. "But I don't want to talk about what can't be changed. I want to know if you can handle what's coming."

Alan looked back over at Joe and took a deep breath.

"He's never going to run for office, is he?"

"Thank heavens, no," Vivian said with a chuckle. "Look at that scowl. That's his normal expression. Can you honestly imagine people voting for that face?"

"Well, I suppose there are worse things than having a former army lieutenant and federal agent as the man responsible for my daughter's safety."

Vivian smiled. "You know what I think? I think once you get to know Joe, you're really going to like him."

Alan glared at her. "Now you're pushing it."

She beamed at him. "I'm going to go find him, and when I do I'm probably going to kiss him, so you might not want to look."

Alan rolled his eyes. "I think I need another drink. Thank heavens for personal drivers."

Vivian left him and made her way to Joe, who had been watching them the whole time.

She reached for his shoulders and leaned up to kiss him on the mouth. His arm tightened around her back for a second, then he pulled away.

"If you're thinking you can bribe me into dancing with you with a kiss, think again. I saw you with Caldwell and your father, both of whom are far better dancers. I won't be left in their dust."

"You came to the hospital," she whispered as she brushed her hand over his cheek. His face, his scowl, all of it was so precious to her.

She didn't try to hide her feelings. She knew they were plastered on her face. It made her feel vulnerable because Joe's feelings were never just out there for the world to see. His feelings were always under the surface, tucked away. Ten years ago it was an exercise for him to hide what he felt.

Except now she knew.

"What are you talking about?"

"That night you found me when I was in the hospital, Daddy…Dad told me you had left. He said you'd been fired and that you left to pack up your things because your assignment was over."

"No," he said.

"No. You came to the hospital. You came to see me."

She watched the memory wash over him. "He wouldn't let me anywhere near you, and I let him keep me away because… I couldn't face what I had done to you. What I had let happen. So I ran. He's right. I was a coward. Of the three of us, you were the only brave one."

"I like that you think those things about me. That I'm strong and brave. When I feel very much like I'm not."

"You are. You were the one who worked up the courage to kiss me at that party. You were the one to tell me how you felt. I can argue with myself all day that the thing that stopped me from admitting the same was my job. But the job was an excuse. I was a coward about that, too. Vivian Bennett, you have always been so much more than me. You're too damn good for me."

Vivian shook her head. "That's not true. If I was able to be brave and strong and survive everything that happened to me, it's because of you. You were my rock, my anchor, always. You were the person pushing me forward even when you weren't there. Any decision I made was because I thought 'what would Joe have encouraged me to do?'"

Joe frowned. "That's not completely accurate. You know I would have told you not to sleep with the douchebag asshole."

Vivian glared at him and then laughed. "Right. I'm pretty sure I did that just to hurt you for leaving me."

"I'm sorry," he said, dropping his head so it rested against her forehead. "I'm sorry I left without a word. I'm sorry I didn't try harder to see you, although in my defense your father did threaten me with arrest at the time. Most of all I'm sorry I was such a damn coward."

"Stop saying that," Vivian said. She almost said *stop saying that about the man I love*. She wasn't ready to go there yet. Not this time. This time, she wanted him to make the first move. To say the words first.

She figured it was only fair.

"It's the truth. I have done nothing in my life to deserve you."

Vivian tilted her head to the side. "There was that one time a crazy man was about to kill me and you shot him."

"Other than that."

Vivian looked into his eyes and saw that he meant it. In that moment it was Joe who looked vulnerable. She didn't believe she had ever seen him like that before.

"When I first came to you again, at the bar, you said I had ruined your life," Vivian reminded him. "I thought you meant because I got you fired…"

He pressed a finger against her lips to silence her. They were in a crowded ballroom. Some people were actually staring at them, as no doubt the rumors of who Vivian Bennett's escort was had circled the crowd. But it felt like the two of them were alone in this moment.

"You ruined my life because for ten years nothing and no one ever came close to replacing what you meant to me. You ruined me… and then you came back."

Vivian couldn't contain what she felt. So

many years thinking she meant nothing to him, thinking he'd been a fantasy instead of a real friend. All that time she'd spent trying to understand her feelings so she could put them behind her. What he'd just told her was Christmas, her birthday and the first day she met Joe all rolled into one.

She beamed. "Then I guess it's a good thing some crazy person out there wants to scare me. Otherwise I might never have seen you again."

"You would have seen me again," he told her.

"You don't know that. It's not the biggest city, but it's entirely possible we would have never run into each other."

"Yes, we would have," he said with certainty.

"Joe Hunt, are you telling me you believe in fate? Because I have to say, that would be rather shocking coming from you."

"No."

He shook his head and looked away from her. As if he was debating with himself. Then finally he took a deep breath and turned back to her. His expression was so intense it nearly made her lose her breath.

"Joe?"

"I knew you were back. I knew where you worked. I went to see your store."

"You came to my store?"

"I lied to you and the puppy this morning. That was me in the picture."

Vivian felt the shock reverberate through her. "You came to my store," she said, trying to put it together. "That photo was dated weeks ago."

He nodded. "I stood outside and watched you try to sell some woman a ridiculous-looking chair. I walked away and I thought about what I would do about it. About you. I told myself it would have to be a random meeting. That we would just run into each other. I told myself I would know the second you looked at me if you had forgiven me for what had happened. Except…it wouldn't have been a random encounter."

Vivian found herself holding her breath.

"I'm a private investigator, Vivian," he said quietly. "It's what I do. You leave your building every morning between eight and eight ten. You stop at the Starbucks near Adams Morgan and get on the Metro from there. Every other Friday on your way home from work, you get a pizza from Frank's Pizza

Place down the street from your apartment. It would have been the most random meeting in the world and I would have planned it down to the second. Except you walked into my local bar before I could make it happen and turned everything upside down. You did ruin my life…but you came back. I had to know if it was too late."

Vivian could feel her heart beating. She'd wanted him to show his feelings, she'd wanted not to be so far out there with hers. She'd wanted to protect herself, but at the same time she wanted *them* so badly she could taste it. And he was giving her that and more.

"You were late, Joe," she told him. "But not too late."

Then she wrapped her arms around him and buried her face in his neck. He held her and said nothing. What a picture they must have presented. The two of them locked together in a roomful of people where Vivian could practically hear the whispers about them.

She didn't care.

She pulled away from him. "Take me home," she commanded in a tone her father would have appreciated.

He nodded and wrapped her hand in his.

She looked around for her father, spotting him by the bar with a drink in his hand. There was a man by his side talking, but Alan Bennett only had eyes for her. She waved to him and he lifted the drink in his hand as a goodbye.

They walked through the lobby, and Vivian felt a sense of invulnerability. As if nothing could touch her, nothing could break her, because Joe was with her. Because Joe had been planning all along to come find her.

But there was one thing she needed to make very clear.

"Joe, I think I know that chair you were talking about. I sold it to Mrs. Eaves maybe six weeks ago, and it was *not* ridiculous looking."

"It had purple flowers."

"It's the height of fashion and it fit her taste."

"Then she has lousy taste."

She stopped and yanked on his hand. "Are we going to fight about this all night?"

He turned to her and slowly shook his head. Then he bent down low so no one walking by them could overhear.

"I told you exactly what I was going to do to you when we got home. Do you remember?"

She did. She really, really did.

CHAPTER EIGHTEEN

VIVIAN GRABBED THE throw pillow she had given Joe as a gift and pushed her face into it to smother her moan. Joe had done exactly as he said he would, so now she was bent over the arm of his couch, her ass tipped in the air, wearing nothing but her high heels, diamonds and…well, Joe.

He was thrusting hard and deep, and she could feel every inch of him as he slid through her wetness. So perfect.

"Oh, please, Joe!"

"You like that? You need it harder?"

"Yes! Please, harder. More. Anything, just don't ever leave me."

Because that's what she really wanted. She wanted him to keep pounding inside her forever so this feeling would never end.

"On your elbows," he growled above her. "Ass higher."

She did as he commanded and immediately

felt the change in the angle. He was so deep inside her, and it only got better.

She felt him reach under her stomach and take hold of her breast, squeezing her nipple hard as his relentless thrusting continued. She wanted to hold this moment. She wanted to stop herself from coming so this would never have to end.

"Vivian," he growled above her as if he sensed what she was doing. "Let it happen, baby."

She lifted her face out of the pillow and turned her head to the side. "But I don't want it to end. Please don't let this end."

He pulled out of her, and the sense of emptiness was so profound she almost whimpered. Joe lifted her up so that her back was pressed against him, his arm across her breasts. As he slid his other hand between her legs, he bent and kissed her neck. Then he rumbled in her ear, "It's never going to end, Viv. But I need to make you come. Do you understand?"

She nodded, but when she started to bend down again he stopped her.

"No, I want to look you in the eyes. I like seeing your face when it happens."

He moved to the couch and brought her

with him. Shifting them both until he was on his back and she was straddling his hips.

"Slowly," he said, his hands on her hips guiding her down over his cock. "I want to watch it happen. I want to see us as I sink into you. I want that memory seared into my brain."

Vivian thought if he kept talking, his words alone would be enough to get her there. Instead she concentrated on positioning him where she needed him to be so that she could sink down on him.

"More," he demanded.

She wanted to tell him that he could really be very bossy, but since more was what she wanted, too, she complied.

Then more orders came. Harder. Faster. Until he was pumping his hips up into her even as she was thrusting down on him, her hands planted on his chest so she could use him for leverage. Finally there was no way to stop it. She was exploding on top of him and squeezing him hard from the inside, and she elicited a sound from him she'd never heard him make before.

It might have been him begging. She'd made Joe Hunt beg. Vivian loved that.

She loved him. She always had. She always would, and she didn't need a therapist or anyone else to tell her why that was messed up. It was simply the truth. A story that started ten years ago.

"Vivian, open your eyes. Let me see you, baby."

She did, and what she saw reflected in his gaze was the most beautiful thing she could imagine. He was groaning, straining and in some ways dying all because of the pleasure she willingly gave him.

Not able to hold herself up, she collapsed on top of his body and stretched her legs out onto top of his. They were still connected, and she tightened her body again around him.

"Viv, you're going to kill me."

She smiled against his chest. "That's in a good way, though, right?"

His hand found her ass and gave it a playful slap. "That's in the best way." Then after a beat he said, "I need to get up."

"Noooo," she cried. She liked this. She liked having her face pressed against his furry chest, knowing that they weren't two separate people but instead one big body mesh.

"Viv, we can't risk…well…uh…leakage,"

Joe said on a chuckle, as if that was the last thing he wanted to bring up.

Because that might lead to a baby. Joe's baby with her blue eyes and his dark hair. And because the idea of it practically made her womb contract, she lifted her head so her chin was in the center of his chest and the words popped out of her mouth.

"Would that be the worst thing? For you?"

He said nothing but stared at her for a long second. Then he gently slapped her bottom again. "Viv, get up."

It hurt, his nonanswer, but she did as he asked and disengaged their bodies, rolling off him and back onto the couch. A couch that wasn't nearly as comfortable as Joe's body.

She watched as he walked away from her down the hall to the bathroom, but the view of his ass wasn't as fun because she decided she very much didn't like watching Joe walk away from her.

Suddenly uncomfortable with her nakedness, she looked around for the blanket he'd covered her with the other night. It was folded on the other end of the couch and, she snatched it up and wrapped it around her.

Stupid. Stupid. Stupid.

She'd put her foot in her mouth by saying exactly what she was thinking, once again making herself vulnerable while he gave her nothing in return. When the hell was she going to learn to check herself and her feelings?

But this led to a whole bunch of other questions about where this was going. None of which she wanted to discuss tonight. In fact, she could have kicked herself for saying anything at all.

Babies! Really? They had been together for a week, a single week, and she was thinking about something as long term as a baby.

She got off the couch, disgusted with herself, and started down the hall. She planned to put her pj's on, start a movie and let him get some sleep. Because while he might think he'd cured her insomnia, there was no way she was going to be able to sleep tonight. Not when she felt so absolutely raw.

Stupid Vivian! Babies!

JOE WAS STILL NAKED, but not worried about that particular fact as Vivian had already decreed she liked Naked Joe as much as Tuxedo Joe. He was leaning against the doorway to his bedroom while Vivian wiggled into a pair of flannel pajama bottoms, the blanket firmly wrapped around her. As if he hadn't made her walk naked across his apartment in nothing but a pair of high-heeled shoes.

And damned if she hadn't been the most beautiful thing he'd ever seen when she'd done it.

Now she had her back to him while she picked up her T-shirt from where she'd folded it on his bed this morning. His time with Naked Vivian was apparently over.

"I was hoping you would sleep with me naked. I like the feel of you pressed up against me with nothing between us."

She whirled around, letting go of the blanket now that she was fully dressed.

"I'm not tired at all. You sleep and I'll watch a movie. Then I'll join you when I think I might sleep. Or I'll just crash on the couch."

Crash on the couch? After what they had just shared, after everything he had told her that evening? Joe didn't think so.

"You're coming to bed with me," he announced.

He pushed himself to standing and walked toward her. He reached for her hand and with the other started pulling down the blankets on his bed.

"Joe, seriously, I'm not tired. I can barely sleep when I am, and I have no shot when I'm not."

"I think we've established you sleep with me."

"Yes, it's been a couple of rare nights—in fact, back-to-back is really rare—but I don't think that is suddenly going to break a ten-year-old habit. You're good, but no one is that good."

"Fine, then stay in bed with me and talk to me for a while until I sleep."

Vivian pulled her hand away from his hold and crossed her arms over her chest. "I don't really want to talk. I certainly don't want to talk about what I just said. It was ridiculous. I shouldn't have said anything about… It doesn't matter. It was crazy talk. I really just want to watch a movie."

"Vivian, please."

She sighed and stomped her foot. Actually stomped her foot like a little girl, and it made him smile. He lifted the covers and she crawled into bed. He wrapped himself around her stiff back.

"Listen to me, Viv. I didn't want us to have a serious conversation during a post-orgasm high. If we're going to talk about making babies, then we're doing it with two clear heads. Okay?"

"Okay. But like I said, it's too soon for that kind of talk anyway," she mumbled.

"Is it? I just told you I spent weeks following you. I had very serious intentions of making something happen between us. Which, by the way, I realize in hindsight telling you I was tailing you for weeks wasn't exactly sensitive considering you're being stalked. Following you like I did might have concerned some women."

"*Some* women don't know you. Tailing me was just your way of getting prepared, and Joe Hunt is already prepared. Too bad that while you were watching me you didn't see the person actually leaving the notes for me."

"We were clearly on two different stalking schedules."

"Clearly," she snorted.

He smiled in the dark. He liked that she accepted that side of him. In fact, he liked that she accepted all sides of him. His stubbornness. His bossiness. She did all that because she loved him, and he wanted her to say it. He couldn't wait to hear those words from her again because he sure as hell didn't appreciate them the first time she said them.

"Do you... Have you ever thought about children?"

Talking about babies was one way to move that conversation along. Because he knew Vivian wasn't thinking about babies without marriage, and she wasn't thinking about marriage without being deeply in love. So he answered truthfully. "No."

He certainly never thought he'd have a chance again with Vivian, and no woman he'd dated had ever moved him enough for him to consider children. The truth was the women he'd dated were a lot like him. A good time, some easy sex and no strings. He could acknowledge now that maybe he'd chosen women like that for a reason. Intentionally stayed clear of anyone who wanted the house-and-family deal.

Because all this time he'd been waiting for her. It sort of made him feel like an ass for Alan to be the one to point out how Joe felt. Then again, he'd spent so much time first trying to suppress it, deny it, feeling guilty all the while, that he imagined his lack of acceptance made sense.

"Oh."

"But I will. Now. I'll think about it hard, Viv."

"Hookay. Well, good talk. Can I get up now?"

"No, let me hold you a little longer, babe. Turns out it helps me sleep. Please."

She sighed. She was a sucker for him when he said please. "Okay."

Joe nuzzled her neck for a bit and then laid his head back on the pillow. Together they lay in the quiet, and he could practically hear her brain racing. His own thoughts weren't exactly calm.

Babies. With Vivian. A son, whom he would raise so completely differently than his father had raised him. A daughter with soft blond curls who called him Daddy with the same love in her voice Vivian always had for her father.

No, he hadn't thought about children before, but he was thinking about it now with Vivian, and there was nothing about it that scared him. Which in itself should have been scary.

He drifted off to sleep. Several hours later

he awoke and Vivian was still there, in his arms, fast asleep.

Yes, he thought. He was that good.

VIVIAN WOKE UP and looked over at the clock. It was almost six in the morning. She'd slept for at least five hours, which meant she was never going to hear the end of it from Joe. She would have liked to have said that it was just the physical activity of sex that was giving her a reason to sleep, but she'd had other boyfriends and none had been able to stop her insomnia.

Then again, she'd never wanted to sleep with anyone after sex. It was always easier to use her insomnia as an excuse to go back to her place, or a reason for him to leave since she didn't have an actual bed.

She quietly got up, making sure not to wake Joe. For a moment she just stared down at him. His face was turned to her and he was breathing deeply and evenly. Relaxed, yet still so very big to her. His presence filled the bed and the room and her every thought. It was overwhelming, but she didn't fight it.

He was hers. This strong man was hers and he'd always been so.

Had he truly cured her of her insomnia? Vivian made her way to the bathroom and looked at herself in the mirror. The dark circles under her eyes were barely there. She would no longer need her thirty-dollar eye concealer to try to hide them.

Was it that simple? Now that she was with Joe, knowing he would never let anything hurt her, knowing he would always be there for her, the underlying fear she'd been living with since the night of her abduction was gone.

These past few nights seemed to bear that out.

She suddenly felt lighter than she had in a long time. Freer. Bolder. Because if Joe was the man who had her back, then Vivian was pretty sure she could do anything.

She made her way back into the bedroom, quietly grabbed some of her clothes and a pair of sneakers and left the room, closing the door behind her. She brushed her teeth, got dressed and went to the kitchen to make coffee. Only to find he was out of coffee.

She knew there was a local coffee place on the corner. She grabbed her wallet and snagged Joe's heavy leather coat, feeling in his pocket for keys. She locked the door on her way out. It didn't really hit her until she stepped onto the sidewalk that for the first time in a week she was physically alone.

Her breath hitched and she forced herself to breathe slowly. In and out. Yes, she was alone, but it didn't mean whoever was sending her those letters was also watching her. Waiting for a chance to strike.

Like Harold McGraw had done.

No, she wasn't going to give in to that kind of panic. She'd lived on her own for ten years, never once allowing her kidnapping to stop her from moving ahead with her life.

Still, Joe would want her to be cautious.

Joe would want her to keep her ass in his apartment until he woke up and could take her to get coffee.

Vivian turned back to the building and considered it. But a burst of anger shot through her. After the kidnapping, there had been that urge to stay tucked in her room, buried under her covers. Joe was gone and her father still had a country to run. As much as he tried to be there for her, he had other important obligations. She could have gone rabbit and never left the protection of the White House, but she'd forced herself every day to go out into the world.

Sure, she'd had Secret Service protection, but it wasn't the same as having Joe. She didn't trust them like she did him, which meant she had to be brave. Funny, she'd never considered that a quality she possessed until Joe had said it. But yes, she had been brave.

Brave to walk the streets of DC. Brave to go back to school. Brave to move on with her life even while she still carried the bruises of her assault.

Some jerk was trying to take that away with a few scary words, and she wasn't going to let it happen. She looked both ways. It was a cold morning and the streets were empty. She wrapped Joe's coat around her and started down the street.

Mission successful, she was back on Joe's floor pulling out his keys while holding the tray with two large coffees in her other hand. She was about to insert the key when the door flew open.

Joe was there in jeans only, his feet bare, a shirt that he'd pulled over his head but hadn't yet straightened exposing his torso.

His expression. She'd never seen anything like it.

Joe Hunt was afraid.

As if he knew what was showing on his face, he closed his eyes and turned away from her.

"I... It was only coffee, Joe. You were out of it."

She set the tray down on the kitchen counter and shrugged out of his jacket. He was standing rigid, his back to her.

Carefully, as if dealing with a wild predator who might strike out, she wrapped her arms around him from behind and pressed her cheek between his shoulder blades.

"I'm okay," she said. "I just went down the street."

She could feel him stiffen, but he nodded.

"I have to...do things on my own... We can't always be together. Not twenty-four/seven. It was just coffee."

"I know," he said gruffly, and he covered her hand resting on his stomach with his. "I just woke up and you weren't there and I didn't know how long you had been gone... I guess I have my own memories I need to deal with."

Vivian circled him so she could look him

in the face. "I'm not taking reckless chances, but we both have to accept that if we can't find who sent those letters, life has to go on."

"It's not an option, Viv. I'm not stopping until I know who is behind this. I get it. You wanted coffee and there's a place not far away, but you don't know if this creep is watching you. You don't. I get what you're saying about needing some normalcy. But not now. Not until I know it's okay to let you out of my sight."

Vivian nodded. He was right. So far they had only been letters, a call and a box of dirt, but she didn't know how far this person would go. As much as her anger had pushed her past her fear, she knew what could happen in an instant.

"Then where do we go from here?" she asked. "You've talked to everyone who might have had some involvement. And you said it yourself, it could be some random person. Maybe someone who knew Harold and knew he used *Sugarplum* as a pet name. He'd obviously used it with his daughter."

"I need to find out where Carl is with the analysis on the dirt and then follow up with Bill to see what he's got on the phone call. I should have heard something by now. Also, it might not be a bad idea to talk with Alice again. Push her a little harder, see what might happen when put under some pressure."

Vivian winced. Hearing the way the woman talked about her father was too unnerving. Still, Vivian would help Joe if it might put an end to this.

He bent his head and pressed it to hers. "Don't worry. I won't make you go back there. You can have lunch with your father or something while I sort it out."

Vivian tightened her arms around him in thanks.

"I don't like her. And I don't trust her. I know it's wrong because she's sick, but I can't help it."

"I know, baby. We'll figure it out. In the meantime our coffee is getting cold."

Vivian looked up into his eyes, seeing his panic was now gone. One moment. One twisted man. It cut both ways, and she finally saw that night from his perspective. How he must have felt when he'd discovered she was gone.

Taken.

"I'm okay, Joe," she told him in a way she hoped he understood.

He cupped the side of her face with his large palm. "Maybe. But I just got you back after ten years. I don't want to wake up without you there again. Okay?"

As lying in bed with Joe was not a hardship by any stretch, Vivian agreed by kissing his cheek.

"Okay. Now we can have coffee."

"Now we can have coffee," he repeated, but she knew what he meant. For now the fear and the panic and the past were gone. She and Joe were just two lovers on a lazy Saturday morning in December who were going to drink their coffee.

The threat of what was out there could be kept at bay a few more hours.

CHAPTER NINETEEN

"WHAT IF THIS person just gave up?" Vivian asked.

It was Monday, and Joe had needed to go into his office. Given it was the holiday season, he didn't have a lot of clients, but he needed to stay on top of what email and phone messages there were. And where he went, she went.

Vivian was right. At the end of all this, they were going to need to go back to a normal life, one where Joe had a small but profitable company to run. Vivian, too, for that matter. As of now he wasn't letting her do any client consultations that involved her going into someone's home. Angela was handling all of it.

He looked over at Vivian, who was sitting in one of the stark guest chairs, shifting around like she was uncomfortable.

"What do you mean 'gave up'?" he asked.

"There hasn't been anything since the box

of dirt last week. And, I suppose, when the planted magazines showed up at your place— if it's even related and your theory of some rogue agent trying to impress my father isn't right. No calls, no letters. Nothing."

"Yeah, because he knows you're with me. But you raise a good point. If whoever planted the magazines wasn't the actual stalker, then the real stalker might still not know where you are. Angela would have let us know if anything showed up at the store, but you have no idea what's back at your place. I'll check it out today. Why are you squirming?"

"This chair is funny," she said. "It's hard and the back is too straight. Is this where people sit when you tell them their spouse is cheating on them?"

"Yes."

"We are so redoing your office. No one wants to hear her husband was out boinking another woman while she's sitting in an uncomfortable chair."

"Boinking?"

Vivian smiled at him and then wiggled her eyebrows. "You know, what we were doing last night. Boinking."

Joe smiled even as he shook his head. He'd

forgotten how much he *liked* her. Now he understood under all that desire and camaraderie, all the banter and fun they had back then, there was something much deeper.

He just really *liked* her. She was goofy, funny and so damn genuine. It was hard to imagine a person who wouldn't like her. Except, of course, for the person who wanted to scare her.

Whoever it was, they were either crazy or an asshole.

"Do you really think hearing that news in a comfortable chair is going to make a difference?" he returned.

"No, but at least she won't be devastated with her butt and her back hurting."

Joe looked around his office. He considered the furnishings serviceable, certainly not fashionable.

"It's the first impression people will have of you when they come in to meet you," Vivian said as if reading his mind.

"You work your clients like this?"

"You're not a client. Most people pay me big money for this kind of advice. Would I be willing to take you on as a client? Sure."

"I'll think about it."

"I'm willing to offer you a twenty percent discount because of, you know…all the orgasms you give me."

He laughed and then lifted his head when he heard a knock on the door. He saw Carl Mather beyond the glass and waved him inside.

"Hey, guys," Carl said, shutting the door behind him. "Just checking in on you two. Making any progress?"

Joe grunted in response. He wasn't making anywhere near the progress he'd hoped at this point. Normally, he was content to let an investigation play out. Let the pieces take him down the path. Didn't matter if that path was a couple of feet or three miles as long as he eventually got there.

This time he wanted this done. Now. He had a life to start living with Vivian. Vivian, who was already talking about babies.

"You hear anything back on that dirt?" he asked Carl.

"No, not yet."

"Can you expedite that?"

Carl nodded. "You know how the lab guys are. Everything in an orderly fashion, but I'll sit on them. I did, however, get the prints back on the magazines. Nothing other than Vivian's and nothing other than hers, yours and her father's on your door either."

"Damn," Joe muttered. "Too many damn dead ends."

Carl held up his hands. "Tell me about it."

"I'm going to head back out to Alice's place. Follow her for a while and see if anything shakes out. I don't like her for it, but I don't see any other options at this point."

"I'm telling you," Carl said, "there is nothing there but a nutcase."

"Yeah, well, I have to do something. Viv, you want to call your father and arrange that lunch?"

"No can do," she said. "I talked to him this morning. He's flying back to China. Apparently things started to break down after he left. They need him back. But seriously, Joe, I can just stay in this office and wait for you. I'll be perfectly safe."

Joe shook his head. "Not good enough. I want eyes on you."

"I'll stay," Carl said. He looked at Joe with a disgusted expression. "Look, I hate it, too. I've got nothing. I have no leads, and no thoughts about what to do next. I want this behind me as much as you do. There is a caseload waiting for me after this. If you think Alice can give you anything, then go for it. I'll hang here with Vivian and make sure she's safe."

"Viv, you okay with that?"

Vivian nodded, but Joe could see something in her expression. "I'll be fine. I really don't want to have to see Alice again, if I don't have to."

Joe looked at Carl. "She's important to me."

"Hey, I get it."

"Viv, you go to the bathroom down the hall, Carl takes you there, okay? If only for my own damn peace of mind."

Vivian got out of her chair and walked around the desk. "Eyes on, got it."

She sat down in his chair behind his desk and settled into the leather. "Now *this* is a chair. Can I use your computer to do some shopping online now that you're officially a client?"

"I said I would think about it."

"Joe, twenty percent discount. What's there to think about?"

He bent down and typed in his password. Then he kissed her on the head and looked to Carl again. "Very important."

"Understood."

"You have my cell. Call if there is trouble, and I'll let you know if Alice leads anywhere. I think I'm going to be a while."

"Yep."

Joe grabbed his coat off the rack near his door and looked back at Vivian. She was already on the internet, apparently intent on finding him some comfortable, fashionable chairs.

"No flowers," he told her.

"Give me some credit," she said without looking up.

He smiled and left the two of them. Ready to go on the hunt.

AS HE WAS driving out to Maryland, his cell phone rang. He didn't recognize the number, but it was local. He answered. "Hunt."

"Joe, it's Bill."

"Bill, thanks. I was just about to follow up with you. Anything on the recording?"

"No."

Joe silently cursed. A background noise, a conversation, anything that might have been a lead. That was all he asked.

"Okay. Appreciate you trying. Especially

given that I was an ass to you." It was sort of an apology, Joe thought. Or at least it was an acknowledgment.

He heard Bill snort on the other end of the line. "You were that. But I think I get it. You and she, you two had a thing back then, didn't you?"

Joe's body tightened. "Something like that."

"Okay, well, here is something. There was nothing I could pick up. Just the clicks of the recordings, which I know doesn't help. But I can tell you this—whoever made that recording knew what they were doing. The room was completely sound free. This isn't some crackpot sitting in his basement with a tape recorder. I mean there was nothing, no sound. Not even breathing in the background. Someone wanted to be sure there was absolutely no chance you would get anything off this tape. That makes me think it's a professional."

Joe thought about that. The break-in at his place had felt professional, too. Nothing out of place, no physical evidence. Just magazines with cutout letters planted in a drawer.

He hadn't even bothered to ask Alan about it because after spending ten minutes with the man, he'd been reminded of the kind of person he was. He might have wanted to separate Joe and Vivian, but he would have approached it differently. Nothing as sneaky as planting evidence.

It didn't rule out his rogue agent theory, but it did limit his options.

And it was another sign of deliberateness.

So he was left with Alice and George, and *deliberate* and *professional* weren't words that came to mind for either of them. Unless they were completely misleading him. He hoped he would learn the truth by following Alice today.

"Okay. Thanks again, Bill. And, Bill… seriously, I'm sorry about what I said. You owe me nothing after this."

"Yep. Well, you owe me. A beer and a burger sometime. Sound good?"

"Yeah. I know a great bar for that," Joe said.

"Good luck with Vivian."

"Thanks."

"She's hot."

"That's enough, Bill."

The other man was laughing as he ended the call. Joe considered the new information. Someone making a recording for Vivian. Doing it in a soundproof environment.

Making sure to leave no audible prints at all. Why? To what end?

Joe concentrated on getting to Alice's place. Surprisingly, someone else seemed to have had the same idea. Joe parked his car and got out. He walked up to the nonflashy sedan and tapped on the window.

Special Agent Puppy Thompson startled, then frowned. Joe made a signal for him to roll down the window.

"You need to get in your car and leave," Thompson told him. "The Secret Service is handling this investigation, and for the record, I still consider you a suspect."

Joe sighed. He hated when he had to admit he was wrong. "You were right. It was me in the photo."

The agent sat up straighter.

Joe came clean. "I heard Vivian was back in town, I went to her place to see her…but I didn't have the balls to actually go inside. Vivian and I…we have history."

"I know about the history."

"No," Joe said. "You don't. I'm not her stalker. I didn't send the letters. I've already told Vivian about the picture. The truth is I… love her."

The kid's jaw dropped, and Joe realized the first time he was saying these words out loud shouldn't be to Agent Thompson.

They should be to Vivian. Another screwup on his part.

"I'm just supposed to accept that?"

"I don't know what else to tell you. It's a fact. Besides, if you're so certain I'm responsible for the threats, what are you doing here?"

"I'm an investigator. I'm checking all possibilities."

It was like he was quoting from the investigation handbook. Total puppy.

"Carl doesn't think there is anything worth following up on with Alice."

"Special Agent Mather and I don't always agree on everything."

Joe nodded. "See anything?"

The puppy finally relented. "No. She left early in the morning, did some shopping and she's been inside the rest of the time. I was just about to move on."

"I'll cover for the next few hours. See if anything pops."

"Where is Ms. Bennett?"

Joe looked at the young agent. "Puppy, is that concern I hear in your voice? If you've got a crush on the former president's daughter, I suggest you lose it."

The younger man's jaw tightened in a way that suggested Joe wasn't completely off base. Vivian's open and honest smile could do that to a man. "I'm simply worried about the subject of my investigation."

"I left her with Carl."

The younger man nodded.

"Hey listen, do me a favor," Joe said. "I already mentioned it to Carl, but if you're heading back to headquarters, see if you can get the lab geeks to move on the dirt analysis."

"What are you talking about?"

"The box of dirt. I gave it to Carl to have it analyzed. It's not much to go on, but it might help with a location. A place to start at least."

"I don't know what box you're talking about. All we have are the letters."

Joe paused. "He didn't tell you about the package that was delivered to her store last week?"

"No. And I met with him about this case this morning. I told him I thought we should stake out Alice McGraw's house, and we disagreed. Truth be told, he said I was being overeager. Said it was just a bunch of letters and a lot of commotion over nothing."

The agent frowned.

"What?" Joe asked, not liking where this was going.

"It's weird. In the beginning Agent Mather was completely amped about it. Making a real case to our ASAC he should be the lead investigator. Figured it was all tied to his history with Ms. Bennett. Trying to make amends or something. Now all of a sudden it's no big deal and a lot of fuss over nothing. And no, he didn't say anything about a box of dirt or anything that had been sent to the lab."

Joe didn't explain. In fact he said nothing. Instead he ran back to his car and got behind the wheel. Peeling away from the curb, he imagined Agent Thompson could hear the screech of his tires as Joe took off. Joe hoped the puppy was putting two and two together because Joe had no time to do the math for him.

He was heading back to DC as fast as he could. He called Vivian's cell and there was no answer. He called Carl's phone and got the same result.

He called his office phone and nothing.

He'd left her with him.

Suddenly it all made sense. The Secret Service had the home videos taken from Alice McGraw. The Secret Service had Rossi's notes.

An agent who had been involved in working the kidnapping case ten years ago would have had access to all of that.

And Joe had left her with him.

VIVIAN STAYED FOCUSED on her breathing. In and out. In and out. She needed to stay calm and deal with the situation. Much like she had ten years ago.

It's okay. Joe's coming.

She really, really didn't like being tied up.

Carl had knocked her unconscious. She'd asked him if he wouldn't mind taking her back to her apartment because she wanted to pick up some more clothes and things from her place to take back to Joe's.

He seemed happy to play the chauffeur. Things weren't exactly easy between them given he'd once thought Joe might be responsible for the letters, but they had been able to find things to chat about. His wife, the decision to put his kids in private school.

So nonthreatening that when Vivian unlocked the door to her apartment she'd been taken completely off guard by the explosion of pain behind her ear. It had shot out through her skull, and she remembered little after that.

Now she was sitting on one of her kitchen chairs, her ankles tied to the legs, her wrists tied behind her back. Her head still throbbed, but at least she was conscious now. Aware of her surroundings and the situation.

"Why are you doing this, Carl?"

He was sitting in the chair across from her, his elbows on his knees, his head down. He lifted his gaze to look at her. He didn't seem like a scary stalker. He looked like a man who suddenly realized his life was out of his control.

"I'm really sorry about this, Vivian. You have to know this was not the plan. But I can't... I don't know what... I'm out of options. You had to go to Joe Hunt. Seriously, Joe Hunt? The one guy I know who will not stop, who will not let this go. Ever. He's relentless. How was that even possible? You two should hate each other."

"We don't."

"Yeah, I get that now," he said, and Vivian

could see he did sound regretful. "He won't go away. I've seen that firsthand. For the three days you were taken, he had to fight to stay on the team, even when your father wanted him off. He was the one who found the property deed on file in McGraw's mother's name to that cabin in Virginia. It's why he was allowed to go on the raid with the FBI. Not that anyone could have stopped him. Which is how I know now…nothing will stop him. Not when it comes to you. And you, you aren't any better. I handed you magazines with missing letters and you didn't even blink."

Understanding finally dawned. Although in Vivian's defense her head still really hurt.

"You sent me the letters."

Carl held his head in both hands, and Vivian saw that in one hand he was holding a gun. Not his government weapon. It was hers. Her small .38. Her father had insisted after the kidnapping that she have a weapon and that she know how to use it. Vivian accomplished both of those things, but it had stayed locked in what she thought was a secure case in her closet since then.

However, the code was her father's birth-

day. Probably not too difficult for Carl to figure out.

"My career for the last ten years has been
shit at the Secret Service. I checked with every
other federal investigative agency, FBI, NCIS,
and none of them would have me. Always that
black freaking mark on my record. The night
you had to become some overwrought college
student who ran away from her protection.
Sure hope whatever upset you that night, it
was something big. Because that one decision
you made cost me a detail with the presidency,
any real career advancement and any chance
to move to another agency. Do you get that?
Do you know what impact that single stupid
act has cost me?"

"I'm sorry," she said calmly. "I really am.
So this was your idea of payback? Scaring me
with some letters? If it gives you any satisfaction, it worked really well."

Carl snorted. "No, this was my chance to fix
everything. I heard you were back and thought
I could have a redo. Send you a few letters,
let you run to Daddy. I could investigate the
case. I had already targeted three scumbag
lowlifes who I could pin for it. Then finally
I'd look like the hero. The guy who saved the

president's little girl instead of the guy who was out back when I should have been out front. Then Thompson gets the wacked idea to talk to Hunt, and I thought…shit. I wanted to stay as clear of him as I could. But I figured it can't hurt, right? If anything it might only make him hate you more, bringing up his mistake from ten years ago and rubbing it in his face. Why doesn't he hate you?"

Vivian took a few calming breaths. She could hear the anger in Carl's tone. The acceptance that his plan had failed and now he was stuck. People stuck in corners either surrendered or they struck back. Clearly, Carl was striking back, but to what end?

"Because he loves me," Vivian said quietly. "He's going to find me, Carl, and when he does he's not going to let you hurt me."

Carl sat up straight, the gun in his hand now resting on his thigh.

"If I thought maybe he would give up I could have made everything just go away. Except now Thompson is convinced it was Joe all along, so he won't stop investigating.

"How did this shit go so wrong? I'm really sorry, Vivian. I have thought of every escape path. I tried to back him off. I tried to back you off. None of it worked. You were still glued to his side wherever he went. I know because I watched."

"Because I love him, too, and I know he would never do that to me. He would never scare me like that."

"You're a naive idiot," Carl spat. "Hell, you trusted me, didn't you?"

Vivian needed to keep him talking. There was a very good chance Joe would try to check in with her at some point. Once she didn't pick up her phone, he would try Carl's. If he got no answer from either of them, he would come back for her. It was only a matter of time.

"You're married, Carl. Your wife is Katie. You have two girls. Mindy and Becca. We were just talking about them on the car ride over to my place. Don't you love them?"

His face turned red. "Of course I love them! That's why I have to do this! Don't you get that? You're dead. Joe is dead. You both have to die or I lose everything! My job, my wife, my kids. It's not going to happen. So when you sit there and tell me Joe isn't going to let me hurt you, you obviously haven't figured it out yet. You're gone. You're both already gone."

Vivian closed her eyes and focused on her breathing. This was different from last time, she thought. Last time McGraw had been crazy. A lunatic. Vivian didn't think Carl was any less crazy. Hatching a plan to make himself a hero at her expense was not rational. But he wasn't a lunatic like McGraw. Carl knew the consequences. He'd taken an action, it backfired and now he knew the life he had with his family was at stake.

He believed his only way out was to kill them both.

For the first time since regaining consciousness, Vivian started to actually fear for her life. He could kill her now, wait for Joe to eventually track her down at her apartment and kill him, too.

Who would ever suspect a Secret Service agent of being behind something as gruesome as a double homicide? Still, it couldn't be easy for him to just kill them and remove all evidence.

"You understand who my father is. He won't let my murder go unsolved."

Carl's face hardened. "He will when he knows it was Joe Hunt who killed you. And he'll have closure, too, because Joe is going to kill himself immediately after. Who wouldn't believe that? You ruined his life, right? Who wouldn't believe he might terrorize you for it, kill you and then take his own life effing *Romeo and Juliet* style?"

Vivian didn't tell Carl that her father wouldn't believe it. He knew Joe wasn't capable of hurting her now. But there was no point. Whatever events were about to unfold, there was no point in talking about it anymore.

"He's coming now," Carl muttered. "Bastard must have already figured it out. Texted me a half hour ago he wanted me to take you to headquarters. Had some information about Alice he wanted to update me on. Saw right through that shit. He knew when you didn't answer your phone something was up."

Joe is coming.

"What did you tell him?"

"He shows up here. Alone. Or you're dead."

Vivian twisted her lips. "Seems to be a theme with you."

Carl turned his head as if he was talking to someone not in the room. "It wasn't supposed to come to this. A few letters, an arrest, the gratitude of a former president instead of his constant derision. It wasn't supposed to come to this."

"I can see that," Vivian said, trying to make him see reason. "You've served your country and your president. Day in and day out you used to put your life on the line for me. You can still be a hero, Carl. Don't become the bad guy."

When he looked at her, she thought her words might have penetrated.

"There is no way out," he whispered.

"I'm the victim of a kidnapping and I survived. There is always a way out."

Except now the conversation was over as someone was pounding on her door.

CHAPTER TWENTY

JOE HEARD THE command to come in from the other side of the door. He turned the doorknob and found it unlocked. He had the irrational thought that Vivian shouldn't leave her door unsecure, but, of course, this was intentional. He stepped into the apartment and carefully shut the door behind him.

Carl stood in the middle of Vivian's living room, a gun pointed to her head.

"You okay?" Joe asked her, his eyes pinned to her.

"Yes," she answered calmly. No panting or short breaths. She was doing everything she could to keep her shit together. His very brave woman.

Slowly he met Carl's gaze. "What are you doing, Carl?"

"Sorry, buddy, this is a bad situation gone wrong, and you and her are my only way out."

"There is no way out, Carl. And you're not

capable of doing this. We both know that. You've spent your whole life protecting the first family. You're not going to put a bullet through the daughter of a former president."

"Does she know about that night?" he asked, and Joe could hear the desperation in the man's voice. Not good.

Joe shook his head. "It was our secret. I never told anyone."

Carl pressed the gun harder against her temple, forcing Vivian's head to bend from the pressure. "It's all going to come out. They'll need to know why I did this, and it will all come out. That night, the college girl giving me head. My wife's going to know... She was freaking seven months pregnant, and now she's going to know. I can't... I can't let that happen. This is the only way."

Joe could see Vivian was confused, but he could also see she didn't really care about what he was saying. She was just trying to keep her cool. Which was all she had to do.

"Okay," Joe said, making sure he kept his distance, his voice nonthreatening even as his heart beat outside his chest. "What's the plan? Shoot her, shoot me? People will hear the shots, the cops will be called. Your hope is they will think this mystery stalker took us both out?"

Carl shook his head. "No, her old man is going to need something more solid than that. Something that makes sense. The one guy he hates more than me is you. He might believe you wanted revenge. He might believe your circumstances twisted you. Murder, suicide. He'll believe that."

"How are you going to do that, Carl? You can't shoot me from any kind of range. You know that. Gunpowder residue is going to have to look consistent, the angle of the bullet will need to be right. One little thing off, and the investigators will know it was staged."

Carl nodded. "Right. So I'm going to need you to take out the weapon you're carrying and put it in your mouth."

Vivian whimpered, but Joe tried to tune her out.

"You think I'm going to shoot myself?"

"It will be easier this way for you. You'll be dead, and you won't have to see me kill her. You do this, I'll shoot her right after. Clean. No pain. You resist me and I'll have to torture her first. You'll have to live through that again. Either way this is going to end with the two of you dead. It's just a matter of how you're going to get there."

Joe reached for the weapon he did in fact have tucked in his jeans. He'd just made it to his office, where he kept a second gun, when he got the text to meet Carl at Vivian's apartment. He took it out carefully and watched Carl tense.

Then he tossed the gun on the floor between him and where Vivian was tied to the chair.

"I'm not going to shoot myself, Carl, and you're not going to torture Vivian. You're going to untie her and you're going to confess everything to your superiors. You tell them straight up you wanted a chance at a promotion. People do crazy shit like that all the time to get ahead. You don't have to tell them about the night she was kidnapped. That does not have to come out. I'll protect your secret. Right now no one has gotten hurt. All you've done is scare her. Yes, you'll lose your job, but you can recover from that. There are a ton of security jobs in the private sector. Shit, you'll probably make more money doing it. This doesn't have to be all or nothing."

Carl closed his eyes as Joe's words sank in.

Then his eyes were on the gun on the floor. Joe watched him put the pieces together. Carl wasn't an idiot. He knew there was no way to pick it up without removing the imminent threat from Vivian. With Vivian not at risk, he knew Joe would take him out.

"Carl, there is no out here other than you putting that gun down and untying her."

"She'll tell her father," he whispered, and Joe knew he had him. "He'll have me arrested."

"I won't," Vivian insisted. "He doesn't need to know about this. I just want it to be over."

"See?" Joe said, holding up his hands. "This isn't horrible. Put down the gun in your hand and take your service weapon out. Put both on the floor and kick them over to me. Then untie Vivian, because I'm sure it's bringing back some really bad memories for her."

Carl still seemed wary, but Joe sensed his panic was abating. The other man could envision the picture Joe was painting. The one where he got to keep his family, if not his job.

"You're not a killer. You're not a murderer. You've served your country well for almost twenty years. Don't let it end this way."

Carl's shoulders dropped. "I didn't want anyone to get hurt. I really didn't."

Suddenly Vivian's apartment burst open. Joe flinched as Agent Thompson kicked open the unlocked door.

"Drop your weapons!" Agent Thompson, who now had his service weapon aimed at his fellow agent, barked at Carl.

Fortunately, Joe hadn't needed to put the pieces together for the puppy. He'd figured it out all on his own. Joe had called him as soon as he got the text from Carl. Two words were all he needed to say.

Vivian's place.

Carl tensed, and for a second Joe panicked. As if the presence of the other agent had ruined Joe's efforts to settle this peacefully. Not taking any chances, he dived forward and knocked Vivian and the chair to the ground, covering her with his body.

"I said. Drop. Your. Weapons."

Carl must have believed the younger officer because after a beat he tossed them to the floor. The situation secured, Joe got off Vivian and brought the chair back upright.

"Did I hurt you?"

"Just untie me," she whispered, clearly desperate to get the ropes off her body. Joe freed her hands and then she helped with her feet as Agent Thompson collected Carl's weapons.

"No one was supposed to get hurt," Carl said. "I wouldn't have… I don't think I could have done it."

"You can explain your actions to the ASAC. Ms. Bennett, would you like to call the police and press charges?"

Vivian glanced at Joe.

It didn't matter to him either way. He would have told Carl anything to make him believe this could end well for him. Including that the police didn't have to be involved.

"Your call," he said.

She looked over at Carl, who was running his hands through his hair. As if he was trying to piece together what had just happened. Joe thought he looked like he'd gone beyond distraught. He looked defeated.

Vivian must have come to the same conclusion.

"No. I don't think the police are necessary. I just want to put this whole thing behind me."

Only Carl wasn't getting off that easy.

Joe took a few steps forward. "Look at me, Carl."

Carl turned his head and Joe pulled his fist back and hit the man under his chin, snapping his head back violently as he fell to the floor.

"What the hell?" Carl asked, reaching for the side of his face.

"That's for scaring her. Now get up and get the hell out of her home. Agent Thompson, I assume you can handle this from here?"

"Yes. I'll take him back to headquarters. He can explain his actions to our boss." The young agent hesitated. "Sorry for...suspecting you."

Joe waved it off. "Guess I can't call you 'puppy' anymore. You were pretty badass."

The kid smiled, then glared at Carl, who had gotten to his feet. "Let's go, Agent Mather."

Head down, Carl left, followed by the junior agent. Joe closed and locked the door behind them.

He turned to Vivian with his heart in his throat. "Are you really okay? I can't believe I left you with him. I left you with him!"

She threw her arms around him. "Oh, Joe, I was so scared, but how could you know? We both trusted him. He was the one who planted the magazines. I understand why he tried to make me think you were behind the letters."

"Did he hurt you?" Joe asked, squeezing her probably too hard. "Because I swear if he did, I will make him pay."

Vivian reached for her right ear. "He hit my head and I blacked out, but I'm okay. It's not bleeding or anything."

Joe immediately took a step back, his hand running gingerly through her hair. He found the lump behind her ear. "We're going to the emergency room now."

"No, I'm fine."

"You could have a concussion," he insisted, checking her eyes for any dilation.

"And if I do, they'll just send me home to rest. Are you sure we did the right thing by not calling the police? I mean, what if his superiors don't do anything to him and he changes his mind and comes back…"

"He's not going to come back," Joe said. "I knew him for years when we worked together. He's not a killer. Trust me. Why he did what he did… He must have panicked when he realized I was going to figure out who was behind the whole thing. Thompson wasn't letting it go on his end, either. Desperate men can do stupid things."

"Stupid things like knock a woman unconscious and then tell her you're going to kill her and the man she loves. Stupid things like that!"

Joe ran a hand over her hair. "I'm sorry he hurt you. Sorry he scared you."

Vivian nodded. "Then you think it's over? Really over?"

Joe wrapped her up in his arms. "It's really over, baby. I promise."

Vivian pulled back and looked at him. "What happens next?"

Joe smiled and placed a gentle kiss on her lips. "I was thinking a quick trip to Vegas. You, me and a wedding chapel featuring Elvis."

Vivian smiled at him. "Joe Hunt, did you just ask me to marry you?"

"I did. I know it's crazy. It's only been a week, but I'm not letting you sleep alone again, because you won't sleep unless I'm there. And I can't have that, so let's make it official. Then your dad won't be so upset when you tell him you're pregnant."

"Deal," she said, and then she kissed him back. "But I was thinking something a little different from Vegas."

Joe looked down at her. "How different?"

Vivian held up her fingers and measured out an inch. "A little different. It's just that I've always wanted Daddy…Dad…to walk me down an aisle."

"Oh Lord."

"With some flowers."

"Please help me."

"And a dress! A really amazing dress."

Joe groaned loudly, but it was all for show. He would move the world to give Vivian whatever she wanted. Even if he had to take out his damn tux again to do it.

Six Months Later

JOE WATCHED HIS bride of three hours take to the dance floor again. He looked around the massive venue and figured everyone in Washington, DC, had come to his wedding. His wedding was the size of a city.

He'd been glad he had those moments alone with her in the front of the church because he was fairly certain it was the last time he was going to see her until he took her upstairs to the suite they had booked for the night.

Tomorrow they were leaving for Paris. Vivian had always wanted to go back, having been once in high school with her father, and Joe was clearly helpless against any request. Evidence of that being he was once again wearing his tuxedo. Because Vivian liked Tuxedo Joe.

Which was why he, and the rest of all the people in DC and probably the outer reaches of Maryland and Virginia, too, were watching his lovely bride be spun around on a dance floor.

She was smiling. No, she was beaming. Not a hint of dark circles lingered under her eyes any longer.

Joe did that. Joe made her happy. It was all he needed in life to feel incredibly accomplished every day.

"Like I said, man, she's hot."

Joe turned at the voice and saw his friend Bill. One of the few people at the wedding he had actually invited. "Hey, man, how you doing?" Joe reached out and shook the other man's hand.

"I'm doing okay, but you're doing very well."

Joe laughed and turned his attention back to his bride. "I am. She's smoking and she's all mine."

Bill laughed and stood with him, his hand around a beer bottle. "Heard from a few people Mather left town. Headed to California, apparently."

Joe nodded. Carl had confessed everything to his superiors. He took the fall for the letters, explaining his attempt to further his career. The service acted swiftly by considering him unfit to fulfill his role.

And Joe had remained silent as promised about everything else. In fact, Joe had been the one to suggest, via Agent Thompson, that a new start for Carl and his family as far away from DC as possible might be a good direction.

He'd done it because Vivian couldn't quite let go of the fear that he might come back for her. It was fair. Carl had made her relive her worst experience. Being tied to a chair, helpless. Thinking back on it, Joe should have hit him a few more times.

But if Vivian wasn't going to let go of the fear, Joe had to make him gone.

"Yeah, I heard the same."

"Crazy stupid-ass thing to do, sending those letters. I suppose it made sense why the recording was so clean. He knew exactly what someone like me would be listening for. What was he thinking?"

"He wasn't thinking." He'd been reacting to ten years of what he felt was unjustified treatment. Resenting Vivian, who had been nothing but a victim, the whole time.

Yeah, Joe really should have hit him a few more times.

"Well, he sure as heck wasn't thinking you would come to the rescue," Thompson said. "Bad assumption."

"The worst."

"You enjoy yourself, Joe. You deserve it. I'm going to go flirt with some bridesmaids."

"Have at it."

"You might want to consider dancing with your wife instead of watching her. I hear she looks even better up close."

Joe smiled and considered the idea of holding Vivian in his arms. While he was not the biggest fan of dancing, nor of being on display for people to gawk at, he found he...missed her. Which was entirely ridiculous but true nonetheless.

He was about to step out onto the dance floor when Alan Bennett caught his eye. Vivian's father made his way through a throng of people to stand next to Joe.

"Hunt," the older man acknowledged. He thought it funny his father-in-law only ever referred to him by his last name when it was just the two of them together. In front of Vivian he was Joe. Alone he was Hunt.

"Alan."

"Are you having a good time?"

"No," Joe answered honestly. "I want all these people to leave and I want to be alone with my wife."

Alan laughed. "I spent a minor fortune on this wedding for you two."

"I would have preferred me and her in Vegas."

Alan huffed. "You would. Thankfully, Vivian wanted something a little more special. Look at her. She's stunning."

Joe glanced over where yet another man, a former senator if he remembered correctly, was now dancing with his wife. He thought about his smoking-hot remark to Bill and decided that was not language Alan would appreciate.

"I suppose I have to give you some credit for that. Half your genes and all that," Joe told him.

"No, all that credit goes to her mother. But when I say it, I don't just mean she's pretty. It's more like she's…"

"Radiant," Joe supplied. Yeah, that was a way better word than *smoking*.

"Yes. She's happy like I've never seen her before. Not since she was a child. As if every shadow has been lifted from her. I suppose I have to give *you* credit for that."

Joe's lips twitched. Not easy words from Alan Bennett.

Alan turned to Joe and faced him directly. "Now promise me this, son. You will not lose her again."

"Never, sir."

"I believe that. Go dance with your bride."

"Yes, sir," Joe said, more than willing to obey that command. He made his way onto the dance floor and tapped the gentleman who was dancing with his wife on the shoulder.

The man didn't need to be asked twice. He simply smiled and allowed Vivian to fall into her husband's arms. Joe wrapped an arm around her waist and cupped her hand in his and didn't try to move them along the floor.

"You hate dancing," she reminded him.

"Yes, but I like the company," he replied.

If it was possible, her smile got even brighter. Alan was right. She was radiant. All her shadows were gone, and he was just arrogant enough to take a little credit for that.

But only a little. She was his brave woman, and she had somehow managed to beat back those shadows.

"When is this going to be over?" she groaned against his shoulder.

"I thought you were having fun," he said, surprised by her question.

"I'm in a corset that is constricting my ribs, a dress that while beautiful is pinching my waist and shoes that while fabulous are making my feet burn with the fire of a supernova. When instead I could be naked, in a bed, with my *husband*. Yes, I'm having fun, but what I want to know is when this fun is going to be over so we can move to the next kind of fun."

Joe bent and kissed his wife, the words *naked* and *in bed* giving him some ideas. "Say the word and we'll put on a show. I'll haul you over my shoulder and carry you kicking and screaming out of your own wedding."

"Really? Now, that's a kidnapping I think I could get behind."

Joe laughed and then was amazed he would ever be able to find amusement in a kidnapping.

"Although," Vivian said as she looked around the room, "I imagine they would think horrible things about you and I've worked really hard to make sure everyone knows what an amazing man you are. Even my father likes you."

It was true. Since Joe and Alan came to terms, they had actually formed their own warped kind of relationship. Two men brought together through the love of a woman.

For his part, all of Joe's family was here, as well. It was sad that his father hadn't lived long enough to see this moment. To see his son truly happy. It might have thawed him a little. Joe was only grateful that at least his father had gotten to meet Vivian. Maybe he'd even heard the love in her voice when she had tried to defend Joe to him.

All Joe knew was that what she'd said was true. Since she'd been back in his life, it had felt like the people who knew his story, who knew their story, treated him differently. It was as if by finally earning her forgiveness, he'd earned everyone else's, as well. When the media had gotten wind of their engagement, they'd received requests from several networks that wanted to do a television special on their reunion.

Needless to say Joe was not having that. Although Vivian liked the idea of the country finally understanding what happened that night and how it was not his fault. Or hers. Joe didn't care what anybody else thought. He and Vivian knew the truth.

"You know your opinion is the only one that matters to me," he reminded her.

She reached up to touch his face, love shining in her eyes. "Back at you, babe."

"You keep looking at me like that and I'm dead serious, Vivian, you're leaving your wedding over my shoulder."

She only smiled brighter.

And that was when it happened. In front of the political elite, her father, his family and their friends.

Joe bent down and lifted Vivian over his shoulder and kidnapped her from her own wedding.

And she couldn't have been happier, if her laughter was any indication.

* * * * *

Get 2 Free Books,

Plus 2 Free Gifts—

just for trying the Reader Service!

HRLP17R2

Get 2 Free Books,
Plus 2 Free Gifts—
just for trying the *Reader Service!*

Get 2 Free Books,
Plus 2 Free Gifts—
just for trying the
Reader Service!